MATRIMONIAL
CAKE

*short stories about
complex relationships*

HAZEL HARRIS

Matrimonial Cake
Copyright © 2023 by Hazel Harris

Tellwell Talent
www.tellwell.ca

ISBN
978-0-2288-9593-0 (Paperback)

She did have a slight tendency to lead, but that could be overcome by a dance partner with strong convictions.

JOHN STEINBECK
The Wayward Bus

TABLE OF CONTENTS

1

WINNIE FROM JAMAICA

Some of this story is true.

Looking down through a thin cloud layer, above the noise and congestion, this post-war British city looks densely packed along its winding waterway. Through the haze, the Thames appears a mucky green colour. On closer inspection, it's rightfully a filthy river filled with the garbage and cast offs from wartime industrials and probably artifacts and armaments from as far back as Hadrian's invaders. And before that, its waters hold the bones and bodies and waste from Neolithic generations.

The sooty and grimey city coatings aren't entirely visible from this altitude but notable structures from earlier centuries are clearly unmistakable. Outlines and silhouettes of kingly architecture soar to very great heights adorned with extravagant facades complete with gargoyles and carved heraldry. Immense green spaces surround palace-like structures and royal-looking buildings like smooth emerald carpets.

But this city is not all rich and grand. Some areas are still damaged or bombed out from wartime aerial invasions. Some areas are downright squalid. Elephant and Castle was one of the hardest hit and by the time of her arrival, many building sites were still rubble brick piles. Much will be written about this period in Britain's history. But for Winnie, as a newly landed Windrush passenger here in London, she is really only concerned with that which pertains to her story.

This afternoon I am sitting in an old movie theatre near Clapham Junction, out of the rain, watching the beginning of the Pathe newsreel in the old Imperial Theater on St. John's Street. Before the lights go out, my eyes will follow the edges of the glitzy art nouveau moldings up, up, up to the impressively domed ceiling. What a gloriously designed old theatre. Previously named The Ruby and even after two renovations, it still manages to inspire awe.

I now sit in the dark waiting for the main feature to begin. How remarkable that this ornate movie house escaped serious wartime shelling, I think. I was told that occassionally it had also served as a shelter during air raids. I had discovered this theatre only three weeks after landing as a stowaway onboard that notable ship, Windrush, which seems to have caused quite a stir in the British newspapers.

The Pathe News as well as the British Movietone News, refers to us women on board Windrush as "ship sisters". I agree. Some of us do feel like true sisters. It is the third such post-war immigration ship to dock at Tilbury but it is the Windrush which seems to have drawn the most attention. The Evening Standard even dispatched an aircraft to capture an aerial photograph as Windrush entered the English Channel. Photographs of our arrival show ecstatic Caribbean migrants crowding the decks and waving to the plane overhead.

Of the 1,027 passengers, 802 are from the West Indies, not the 482 as mentioned in the newsreels and 15 are stowaways (of which I am one), not the eight recorded by the Tilbury Gazette and finally 66 Polish Nationals who are part of a Resettlement Program to Britain. The remainder are passengers returning to England post-war.

And on that happy landing day, June 28,1948, the sun seemed to struggle to shine but my stowaway heart felt extremely light.

Now the weather forces me indoors on stormy days. When the rains came I looked for shelter in tea shops until I remembered this theatre where tickets are bought outside under a gaudy marquee. Once seated, we Windrush passengers are caught on film by the Pathe and Movietone newsreels which have eagerly recorded our arrival. The Windrush has been the subject of important news over and over again, showing our landing and her official welcome to England's shores. It's wonderful to see those familiar men and women gazing into cameras showing their wide happy smiles. All the pictures display our handsome faces in the best possible way: young, eager, adventurous, optimistic. And if our arrival wasn't enough, updates on our daily lives since landing are filmed repeatedly. The public can't seem to get enough of us. Our faces light up the big screen, foreheads three feet wide, noses two feet long.

The Pathe or Movietone Newsreels are the most intriguing sources for current post-war information. Impressively narrated by deep male voices and with the stunning visual effects of 1948 movie technology, the dramatic stories of WW2 experiences, Nazi resistance and the heroes of wartime fill the screen. Four years after the end of the war, its repercussions are still replayed over and over in hundreds of theatres all around the world. Four years later, fragments of that horrific era are still front and centre on a daily basis. Four years later, stories like the Windrush and its passengers remind the world that life goes on.

My remarkable destiny as one young Windrush passenger will be "forever changed" according to the Pathe news. I have unwittingly become the centerpiece in an elaborate story which describes me as a pretty, young Jamaican stowaway befriended on board by a rich British woman named Nancy Cunard who is the heiress to the famous Cunard Shipping fortune. And today, as I look up at the screen, I see my enlarged face smiling into the camera for all the world to see. My face. If only my three Jamaican aunties, my mother and my granny could be here with me now. I have shared my exciting arrival news with them in several letters and can well imagine their raucous reactions. How they would laugh. "Oh, dat Winnie," they would say to each other, clapping their hands and slapping each other on the back.

I was one of several stowaways who had sneaked aboard the Windrush sailing to England. The boarding area was congested and noisy which served my purpose well. I had managed to sneak on board as the Windrush departed Kingston, Jamaica before it made a brief stop at Port of Spain, Trinidad and then Tampico, Mexico. What surprises me is that I was able to do everything in plain sight.

I told the ship's purser, in a frantic voice, "I've just been separated from my husband, only seconds ago . . . I let go of his hand. There he is, look . . . up ahead. I can see him waving to me. He has my papers . . . see . . . and my boarding pass."

"Fine, go forward," said the boarding agent. And that was that.

Two weeks before the departure of Windrush, I had been one of hundreds of Jamaicans who had read in Kingston's Daily Gleaner newspaper of this remarkable opportunity. Cheap transport was available for returning military personnel from the British West Indies to the UK. For me, it wasn't just a sudden impulse to leave Jamaica which propelled me forward. I was searching for something much grander outside of the grinding poverty which was all the women in my family knew. This chance appealed to many of us who wanted a better life, better opportunities, a better job.

The demand for tickets soon far exceeded the supply but that didn't seem to stop me. I was told I was crazy. I was told I had no military connection as a wife or relative but that didn't seem to stop me. I also had no money but even that didn't stop me. I was told that even if I had the money I would face a long queue to secure passage. I was leaving everything and everyone I knew but even that didn't seem to stop me. I had never been so driven. I had barely four British pounds saved and only one week to enact a bold stowaway plan.

WW2 and the military presence in the West Indies had had a huge political influence on our lifestyle. Prior to this period, Jamaica, Trinidad and Tobago were still emerging from a post-plantation society. Government pronouncements were still broadcast to the population by loud speakers hung in trees. Although there was an abundance of automobiles, the main method for transportation was still by donkey cart. Silent movies were just passing out of favour. Many ex-servicemen from the British West Indies jumped at the opportunity to return to Britain with the hopes of either finding good employment or re-enlisting in the RAF. Some just wanted to see "what the mother country looked like".

During the day I mingled with the other passengers and danced to the buoyant calypso music. There were so many musicians aboard and the steel pans were a-throbbin'. I would cadge food from a few of the sympathetic servicemen whom I trusted with my secret passenger status but at night I slept on the open deck wrapped in my sweater, a scarf and a small lap quilt made by my mother as a parting gift. When I was found-out by the ships' officers along with the other stowaways, the "whip-round" raised a portion of the money needed for our £48 fares. Newly discovered, the goodwill of the captain and crew allowed us stowaways to continue sleeping in our deck chairs during our 30 day crossing. The camaraderie and joy in knowing of such support was remarkable, especially since the customary alternative would have been the brig.

This was where Nancy Cunard discovered me, shivering in my deck chair one dewey early morning, three days after departing Kingston. I had noticed her previously, doing her calisthenics on my deck but had always feigned sleep. On this particular morning, she suddenly appeared beside my chair loaded down with a large blanket and proceeded to cover me up. I was both overwhelmed by her generosity and suspicious of her kindly act since she had singled me out amongst the other stowaways with this thoughtful gesture.

Nancy seemed excessively drawn to me. She was a strange sort of woman and not the type I would have ever been inclined to befriend. It surprised me how insistent and needy she seemed whereas I was clearly the needy one. Perhaps in taking me under her wing she satisfied a need to be seen as a good samaritan. Who was I to turn away from such a helping hand?

Nancy had not hidden the fact that she came from money and displayed a careless disregard for whatever it would cost to upgrade my shipboard status. I turned down her cabin invitation which became the first sign of discord between us. I knew I was in no position to reject her hospitality but her insistence to be seen as my rescuer began to grate. Since I continued to sleep overnight in my deck chair, I knew this rankled her further but I saw no other solution. To counter my perceived lack of gratitude, I felt a need to constantly placate her. I realized I had to spend time in her company so I happily dedicated early mornings to watching while she did her exercises and then we'd have breakfast. When I accepted a seat at her dining table, I saw how proud she was to show me off. At first she seemed uncomfortable displaying her philanthropy so publicly. She showed a very shy kind of humility, always lowering her eyes to avoid further admiration. I saw this repeatedly since all the passengers and crew had become aware of my situation. It was common knowledge that I was "one very lucky girl".

Her humility seemed to evaporate, however, when I showed preference for being with my other stowaways and countrymen. I would gravitate back to my fellow Jamaicans for the jovial kind of company I craved because I was making wonderful new friends amongst all the Caribbean passengers. One sweet fellow, Alvin, called me "Winnie-Rush" which provided us a great laugh but I noticed Nancy was slow to acknowledge this nickname as a worthy joke. Even though I always invited her to join us, she would become immediately silent and withdrawn. She often left our group gatherings voicing some excuse. She would then sit off to one side casting furtive glances in my direction.

She told me she wanted to know everything about me. When I started with stories of my family life and my many aunties, she would interrupt with her thoughts on "all the privileges" she felt I had probably missed growing up. Or she would appear bored and stare back at me with glazed eyes. When I inquired about her background, she would avoid my questions, telling me there was no one left in her family of any consequence. She described her relationship with them as more of a business arrangement.

It was into our second week of travel when she asked me to consider following her on her international trips. She represented her family's Cunard Shipping Line and her job was to deal with global transport contracts. She had been reading an old newspaper at the time and took it out to illustrate something of her professional responsibilities by referencing one of the headlines. And when I pointed out a written comment from the front page, Nancy couldn't hide her shocked look of surprise in discovering I was literate. "You can read," she said simply, staring at me with unblinking eyes.

"Yes, and I also have a fine written hand," I added. "Thanks to the Catholic Sisters Of Great Benevolence. We're not all jungle savages, you know."

Nothing except a long silence now hung between us.

"You could perhaps become my traveling companion. Or, how would you like to accompany me as my secretary?"

She was actually offering me a job. I would have a chance to see the world. I could enjoy a kind of gracious living which for someone like me . . . I'm not sure why I found her patronizing tone so offensive but I left the dining room after that conversation and avoided her company until the following morning.

If we were to look at what we shared, our common ground was sparse. Other than a mutual love of movies and the fact that we were both born on the 5th day of our respective birth months, I could see no similarities. She found that tiny bit of birthday synchronicity to be very compelling. I took it as the only sign of a flimsy bond with an overbearing woman.

Upon landing, I was seized by the police along with the other stowaways and incarcerated in detention for two weeks. I knew I was taking advantage of Nancy's affection by asking her to provide the legal counsel for all of us as a group. It helped our cause that the newspapers were following my stowaway story closely. I knew it would reflect poorly on her if she revealed a less than generous inclination after we had docked and legal proceedings had begun. With her considerable wealth and influence, she appealed to the judiciary for us as hardship cases. We were each fined £1 for the charge of travelling without payment and an additional £1 for being a stowaway. We all thanked Nancy profusely in providing payment for those of us who couldn't afford the fine. Otherwise, non-payment would have meant receiving concurrent sentences from Greys Magistrate Courts. It was all very intimidating. At least we weren't sent back to the West Indies. That would have been a horrid return for many of us.

Our two weeks in detention was then followed by the well televised event of our release. Amidst all the reporters screaming for attention and exploding camera flashbulbs, Nancy waited for me curbside in a taxi. She had just come from a BBC radio interview where she announced I was being released by the British judiciary as a legally landed immigrant. Nancy, having singled me out as her "ward" was continuing her happy drama played up by all available news sources. At this point, I realized I needed to clarify my position once again. I felt badly that it wasn't to be the expected "happily ever after" that she and the world were waiting to see.

Nancy failed to understand the significance of how it would make me feel if I were to take up her many offers. I felt oddly like I was deserting my other stowaways as we were now quite a close group. We had become a tight little community, especially in detention. I knew I really owed them nothing past negotiating for our release, but felt in my heart that I would be starting my new life in the UK by taking an unfair advantage. My good fortune had required absolutely no skill on my part other than appealing to Nancy's vanity. I could hear my aunties telling me, "Winnie, you be right in what you feel if you tink dat little bit o' self-serving will catch you up by de troat sooner or later? . . . den you bettah be listen to dat voice in your head."

Nancy was not happy with the solidarity I showed my fellow stowaways and spent much effort trying to convince me of the many options she was laying at my feet. Granted, my good fortune in meeting her was a genuine stroke of luck. I knew that and again expressed my gratitude. Could we not simply remain as friends? Why was it such an "all or nothing" choice for her? She seemed to demand that I choose her over everything else. I had never realized, in all my years before leaving Jamaica, that I possessed such a strong independent streak. Eventually, she turned her back on me and "damned me all to hell" for the trouble she had taken regarding my plight.

"Go your own way then," Nancy barked. "See how tough it will be without my help to be a black woman in a white man's England."

Winnie now stands by her bed in the temporary deep shelter at Clapham Junction, a part of the Northern Tube line that is being used to house Windrush immigrants. Tomorrow, she will head back to the Labour Exchange in Brixton to scan new postings for domestic work.

When the ship docked in June, the memories of that wonderful day coloured all her feelings about England. Even through the fears of detention and possible further incarceration she had felt buoyant. Even through her squabbles with Nancy, she had felt optimistic. But now it's into September and the rains are constant. She is thankful for her South Clapham shelter which is available for another month. It has not been the ideal lodging but was provided free to unhoused Windrush immigrants for three months. As well, she has made two close friends in Molly and Alvin.

She knows if she had a window to look out, she would see only drizzly streets. No need just to watch cars and people passing. Or to feel spitting raindrops against her face. Winnie's arrival has now become overshadowed with the daily expectation of London's constant downpour.

She still ruminates over her conflicts with Nancy. Nancy, rich and privileged. Nancy who underestimated her ability to make her own choices. Nancy who had shown little interest in knowing anything about her life. Why was she never curious about my Jamaican childhood? My aunties and my mother? My granny? My friends? What was I to her? Just a new project? This awareness only makes Winnie fiercely miss her endless Jamaican sun, its turquoise waters, street sounds, joyous music, the comfort of overhearing her grandmother Mary and her mother Lucinda chattering with the invisible *duppies* in the kitchen while cooking. This is Winnie's first time realizing . . . she is homesick.

Winnie's own family history has survived on memory and myth. She is descended from a long line of those Jamaicans who practice Obeah. They are the women and men who use voodoo and rasta and their magic makes them exceptional. Before her grandmother Mary's time, the stories that Winnie knows of her lineage have been cobbled together by her three aunties and her mother. With every telling and retelling, the added personal embellishments sometimes result in a whole new story.

And still, many of their current practices remain immutable. For example, no one amongst Winnie's family would ever question the value of burying the umbilical cord of a newborn under a newly planted tree. What better way to connect a child to its homeland. Or, to occupy a new house demands the blood of a beheaded chicken or goat to be sprinkled on all four corner posts. Just like the one-sided conversations that occupied Winnie's granny whilst she scurried about her house, those same *duppies* can sometimes be evil and cause troublesome mischief. All of the women in Winnie's family know with certainty that multi-coloured clothing confuses the bad spirits and prevents them from following a straight path to bedevil you. These kinds of beliefs have bonded Winnie's aunties and mother tightly; they are proud of this strength. They can prove their magical abilities in many instances. After all, there were often many witnesses to seemingly inexplicable events which led observers to suspend disbelief about Winnie's family's supernatural abilities.

Winnie knows this power runs through her line from the men and women before her. She can trace her mystical origins as far back as the woman they have come to know as Morowa . . . who was rescued by Otembe who was followed by Akuba who was followed by Shanti and then Shiloh . . . and then . . . and then. The list of names becomes a rhythmic poem. It travels down through many names, both men and women, until it reaches Winnie's grandmother Mary and her four daughters Simone, Lulu, Mabel and Winnie's mother, Lucinda. Then it stops at her own name: Winnifred.

The origin of Winnie's family stories goes like this: Morowa arrived in Jamaica as a captured slave from Togo or Benin. Auntie Lulu has always questioned that fact. Morowa's exact origins are uncertain but Auntie Lulu is convinced she was of the Ashanti people from Ghana. On her forced march west to the Atlantic, Morowa is twice held in slave centres as the Portuguese raiders added more captives on their trek to the ocean. There, she was sold to a British slaver for transport to the West Indies. At the time of her capture, Morowa is four months pregnant.

Now, newly arrived in Jamaica, Morowa is being prepared for sale. She has lost every vestige of her royal bearing when she is hoisted onto the auctioneer's platform with the other captives. Her legs are weak and her skin is ashy. Her face has been oiled to appear healthy. The hardships of unspeakable unsanitary conditions on the slave ship have left her emaciated and covered in flea bite scabs. She has long ago lost the carved ivory and gold pendant from around her neck which had been placed there by the king himself during their binding ceremony, a long time past. Little did Morowa know of the king's scheming second wife who had arranged for her capture by the slavers.

My name will be Morowa when I become the third wife to the king. It holds a special meaning for him I am told. Hopefully, as his new bride, I will prove to be of notable fertility. He will love me as his special wife, I know. I am lithe and long and supple. What man can resist that? My skin is like black lacquer, soft and smooth, unwrinkled. One day I will be old and withered but for now I am polished and strong-limbed. My feet are large and my toes splay easily which makes me useful for walking long distances. Straight strong toes, the king says. Good. I'm like the tree dwellers that use their feet like hands. The king sees me when I am just a girl and tells a servant woman to send word to my father. She is told to notify the king when I am ushered to the women's hut for my bleedings.

Morowa stands now before rude men pulling at her lips to check her teeth. Unshackled, her arms are lifted to show her muscles. They rudely indicate a need for her to spread her fingers to show strength and dexterity. Because of her distended pregnant belly, she is boastfully paraded across the platform as "two for the price of one". She is to be purchased for about 250 British pounds to work in Jamaica's cane fields.

It is at this precise moment in the history of early 18th C. Jamaica, that a powerful earthquake strikes this small port settlement. Almost two-thirds of coastal Port Royal is built on a sandy spit which immediately plummets into the sea.

After a most horrific sound which I can only liken to the roar of many jungle animals, I find myself scrambling for any means to prevent drowning. I am suddenly under several feet of ocean and can see many chained captives fighting to swim to the surface as I am. What has happened? Thankfully unencumbered, I break through the turbulent waters and stagger to gain a foothold amidst the screams and shoutings from everything around me. When I turn, I watch with great wonder as a mountainous wall of water begins to build far out to sea. I see everyone running as fast as they can away from this water wall. It is like nothing I have ever heard or seen. Cradling my large stomach, my hand is now taken by a fellow captive who makes me run even faster than I am able.

We run through the night to keep ahead of the great water surges. Knowing no direction to follow, we continue inland, climbing higher, hoping to find refuge from the waters and recapture. While we crouch to drink from a mountain stream, I can see his heavily carved facial tattoos reflected in the moonlight.

Auntie Lulu's continues the story like this: *I am Akuba, the granddaughter of Morowa. I am the girl child . . . of the girl child . . . whom Morowa birthed after reaching an inland encampment of escaped slaves here on the island of Jamaica. The original story of my grandmother, Morowa, has been carefully told and retold to me by my mother. She had it memorized and now it belongs to me. I must guard this story and keep it safe for my own daughter because that is how she will know of our special magic.*

I am proud of my name: Akuba. It is Ghanian and means Wednesday's Child. We are practitioners of Obeah, a mysterious ability to create destiny and good fortune through spiritual healing. We are also capable of creating great misfortune for those who oppose us.

Today, I have come to see my Grandmother Morowa because I may be pregnant. Descending from Obeah women has given me many powers. One of those powers is to see my own destiny and the destiny of others. I saw my own mother's death from a scorpion bite when I was just a little girl. I had a dream one night and when I awoke, I called out to her to be careful where she walked. I knew she was heading out that night to harvest the juice from a certain plant which can only be milked under a full moon. She must have felt so abandoned, lying alone in the jungle unable to call out as the paralysis crept through her body. My grandmother Morowa and I buried my mother in our traditional Nine Nights customs.

Many villagers had gathered with us for our Nine Nights following my mother's death. She and I had happy years together before that scorpion found her foot. She was a proud Obeahwoman, an important voice at our gatherings. Through Obeah, we know we can resurrect her spirit.

My favourite view of GranMama Morowa's little house is from a hill overlooking her rickety back porch. From this hill I can just make out a well worn jungle path leading to where she keeps all her medicines, charms and potions. Scores of little containers hold a wealth of natural pharmacopeia gained from the surrounding jungle. Everyone comes to GranMamaMorowa for help when they are ill or bothered by chaos. It was said her magic had been recognized immediately, many years ago, when she and Otembe accidentally found an encampment of run-away slaves who called themselves Maroons. This encampment was one of many such small inland Maroon settlements. My grandmother Morowa and her rescuer Otembe came to realize it was through their powers of Obeah that they had miraculously stumbled into such an encampment.

Auntie Simone continues, *"Over the years, preceeding that particular earthquake catastrophe, many scores of run-aways had created small mountain settlements in the interior of Jamaica island. None of these ex-slaves shared a common language but all were united in fighting the British slavers, a common enemy. They fiercely protected their new-found independence just as fiercely as the British fiercely fought to restore colonial order."*

Auntie Mabel picks up the story like this: *"There is a lingering hostility toward our family because of one of our young men named Shiloh, who was the son of Shanti who was the child of Akuba. Shiloh . . . he helped the British authorities recapture run-away slaves. He was one of the many slave troops enlisted to fight alongside the British in exchange for his freedom. That was many many years ago but the Jamaican memories of Shiloh's treachery are long."*

Auntie Simone adds, *"Several attempts were made to annihilate our Maroon population. These little Maroon villages are still numerous which is a testament to the courage of run-aways. Obeah is very powerful with us Maroons and was often thought by the British to be the strongest influence in persuading us to revolt."*

Winnie remembers these tellings many times throughout her childhood. The women would sit around their kitchen table stitching on pieces of needlework and while they sewed, they would tell Winnie of her history.

"I could have explained all of this to you, Nancy, if you'd been even remotely patient or wanted to listen," Winnie says aloud.

But you weren't interested in my story, she thinks. What were you afraid of? If I was home now with my aunties and my mother, they would be tempted to send a devilish spirit to bother your sleep or trouble your mind with disturbing confusion. Granny would make your hips stiff so you would have difficulty walking. Just say the word, Auntie Lulu would tell me. Just say the word, Winnie-girl, and we can make her hair turn white overnight.

Today, the movie house is again Winnie's escape from the confines of South Clapham deep shelter. She sits up front, close to the screen with Molly and Alvin. After Nancy's departure became public information, the Movietone News, the Pathe Reels and the other news outlets had all turned their attention and their cameras toward newer more compelling human interest spectacles. Winnie's story no longer captivates.

Winnie begins to imitate a deep narrator's voice, supplying the commentary by speaking in a low register, saying, "The sad fact is that Nancy Cunard's remarkable opportunities were rejected by young Winnie from Jamaica. She has disappointed all of us here in London who yearned for a faerie tale ending to this incredible stowaway story. Here we see the sorry result for "one very lucky girl" from the Windrush. Winnie is now just one more Caribbean immigrant struggling to make a new life in a foreign city".

"Okay, Winnie, now you stop that nonsense," laughs Molly, "That's enough now. Everything will work out for you right fine. You'll see."

"Yes-s-s, Winnie-Rush, we all be in the same soup together," says Alvin. Look at you . . . even in the dark, you burn bright."

Soon, several others from the shelter have spotted Winnie, Molly and Alvin. They quickly move to the front of the theatre in order to sit as a group. These were the same Windrush friends who had waited outside the detention center when the stowaways were released at the end of July. On that day, Winnie and the other stowaways had caught sight of these friends waving their large Jamaican flag above the heads of the inquisitive reporters and all the blinding camera flashes. Their release was written up in the papers as: "Joyous Jamaican Hullabaloo". The many photographers made such a commotion that Winnie and her friends had a hard time finding their way through all the noise and chaos. It was then that Winnie was ushered into a waiting taxi by Nancy.

An hour later that same taxi made an abrupt stop at the doorways leading down the stairs to the South Clapham deep shelter. Nancy had finally exhausted all her unsuccessful persuasions and ordered Winnie out of the cab. Winnie then watched as Nancy was driven away without even a backward glance.

Today is the 5th of April and Winnie's 55th birthday. She is waiting for her three married children to arrive so the birthday celebrations can begin. Winnie sips a glass of beer while watching the calypso band setting up in one corner of the restaurant. Alvin is in the kitchen, supervising at the stoves, preparing the birthday food. He keeps mischievously poking his head around the corner to wink at his wife and make her laugh.

She sits thinking back on her Windrush experience. Hard to believe she has lived in the UK for 35 years. Windrush was a remarkable time in her life. And the fact that it had been captured on film newsreels and shown in theatres all around the world is still amazing to her after all these years.

Her courtship and marriage to Alvin occurred a year and a half after arrival. They had originally set up house in a little rental flat in Notting Hill which became a popular area of London inhabited by Caribbean immigrants. Winnie grew to love her street because of the noisy buoyant joy which sounded like the Jamaica she had left behind. It seems only natural, she thinks, that out of that small West Indian community, the famous Notting Hill Caribbean Festival has grown to such an extent.

Since their marriage, Alvin had worked on the trains as a porter for twenty-five years before he opened his "Jerk Chicken Caribbean" restaurant with two friends. Winnie had originally found employment as a domestic worker until she became pregnant with the first of her three children. The following decades saw them moving twice as their flats became more cramped.

———•———

When Winnie turns 60, she returns briefly to Jamaica with Alvin and their children. She walks through what is left of her little Maroon village and talks with a few older people who have memories of her as well as her mother, her three aunties and her grandmother. She remembers how exciting it was for all five women when they moved to Kingston to have a chance at a better life. It was only through their clever needlework skills that the women in her family were able to put food on the table.

Shortly after Winnie's 70th birthday, her eye is caught while watching a televised news story showing the christening ceremony for a new ship of the Cunard line. An aged and frail-looking Nancy is seen, unsmiling, standing on a dais before a microphone, announcing this momentous launch. Winnie continues to watch as Nancy unleashes a large champagne bottle which swings out and crashes against the hull of a massive transport vessel at the Tilbury docks.

Everything good in my adult life has come from that stowaway decision. I have made my own destiny, she thinks to herself. I have created my own good fortune.

2

THE ANCIENT ROMAN EMPIRE

The Circus Maximus was built to hold 250,000 spectators on four levels of marble and wooden seating. It was an oval track, 600 m long (roughly three football fields) which ran around a long, raised, colonnaded strip called the spina. The spina held course markers, statuary in honor of the gods (inherited from the Greeks) and royal tributes to the current emperor.

Margot leaves off reading her pamphlet and hastens her walking pace. She needs to catch up to her travel group which is readily identifiable by their bright green lapel buttons issued at the airport. Their guide also holds a bright green flag to which he has attached his bright green umbrella. Margot is on the "Ancient Rome's Highlights" segment of her 21-day European tour.

". . . and over the thousand years of this Roman spectacle, every racing day began with the entry procession led first by . . . " continues the guide.

Margot can only half focus through all the surrounding distractions. Another tourist group walks past, carried along by the loud, over-the-shoulder voice from their guide speaking what sounds like, perhaps Russian? She is as intrigued by these foreign sounding words as their questionable choices in travel fashion.

She soothes herself, thinking, "How **would** John have managed with all this? He'd probably have ended up either making a daily list of language corrections for our Italian guide or stomping off in a great huff to be by himself. It's better that I'm on this tour by myself. At least I don't have to deal with his embarrassing tantrums."

Margot has been married to John for twenty-five years as she presently ponders her life, here, on this vast empty field in the ancient heart of modern-day Rome. She remembers a rush of lustful admiration for his physique which now seems completely irrelevant. Her feelings for him have long since been overshadowed by the constant dread of his endless, endless negativity. Still, she marvels at the attraction she initially felt for this man . . . his magnificent hands and forearms . . . and with his shirtsleeves rolled up . . . and that rugged wristwatch . . .

His parents were extremely proud of their well-spoken, academically-inclined son. As Latvian immigrants, they often told her they needed their son to speak perfect English, thereby reflecting their own desire for assimilation. For themselves, they would stumble along with broken words and phrases but their son would demonstrate full respect for the country which had so graciously provided them asylum.

John's father, Ivan, had worked three menial jobs after immigrating, saving diligently over the years to buy a house and when their first-born arrived, and it was a boy, their joy knew no bounds. Their chosen country had indeed blessed them.

Margot met John when she enrolled in one of his history classes as a prerequisite for her own teaching degree. His very youthful appearance belied the fact he is 15 years older, which, when she discovers this (inexplicably seductive to her) age discrepancy, only makes her redouble her efforts.

He introduces Margot to his parents and summarizes his attraction for her by stating she is not part of that "cloyingly infantile coquetry on constant display in the front rows of my lecture theater". Bespectacled Margot needs to sit close during classes because of a troubling short-sighted astigmatism which has rendered her a lifelong wearer of glasses.

Later, as they leave his parents' home, he assures her, "I meant you seemed quite unlike the other students your age, Margot. More settled, more mature. All those silly Barbie dolls with their bleached hair and low-cut blouses . . . " A mocking scoff follows.

"But, in terms of physical attraction, John, was it just something I was . . . **not**?"

"You looked sensible. Intelligent. Thoughtful. I liked that."

"I'm asking you, John, what is it about me you find attractive?"

"Well, you always look at me directly . . . and you consider your answers carefully before speaking,"

"I guess I want to know if you find me **physically** attractive, John. I feel foolish fishing for compliments."

"Then don't. It doesn't suit you. That's not who you are."

Margot turns back to her pamphlet: *During the great chariot spectacles (500 BC - 400 AD), sentries needed to be posted throughout Rome to prevent vandals from looting and engaging in destructive acts. The city was left largely empty, thereby presenting enticing opportunities for vandalism.*

Their guide is now pointing to the remains of the royal palace overlooking this immense empty field which once held the racing track. Margot lets her eyes trace its outline against the afternoon sun. Her group stands in a tight little circle intent on their guide's descriptions, but Margot finds her attention caught by certain members in her tour group.

These eleven traveling companions have been with her since their meeting at a designated rendezvous point in Heathrow's airport. It seems like only yesterday. Margot is the solo traveler on this tour, and because of this, she pays extra for single sleeping accommodation. The group is composed of Margot, four couples plus one threesome of giddy Dutch girls who laugh constantly at their own private jokes.

Their itinerary has so far covered a drive north from London to Hadrian's Wall followed by a few days south in Bath. On their return to London, two days are spent touring early Londinium. Next, they fly to the south of France to view Roman ruins in D'Avignon followed by a flight to Tunisia to walk the remains of Carthage. Margot is extremely taken with Tunis' Bardo museum where its bright white walls display an impressive number of tiled mosaic floors from early Roman villas in North Africa. A short trip out into the Tunisian desert is included to visit a well preserved colusseum. And now, a visit to Rome itself.

Margot has always been intrigued by archeology, ancient dig sites and history but her enthusiasm pales in comparison to John's. His post-graduate degrees, received at an impressively young age, are part of what ensures his position in academic circles. He devotes much of his spare time to historic research and knows his attainment of tenure will soon be a sure thing. Yearly, he produces a new academic paper and is constantly sought as a notable guest speaker. So, when Margot suggests this 21-day tour, Highlights Of The Ancient Roman Empire, she thinks he will be thrilled.

At first John remains quiet, almost dumbstruck. What follows, after his mocking snort, is not anticipated.

"And how do you think I could tolerate, knowing what I know and having to hang onto a guide's half-assed explanations on subjects for which I am, **myself**, internationally acclaimed? I'm the one who should be leading these tour groups. My god Margot, how little you know me."

"Well then, why don't we set our own itinerary? Just the two of us. And you could be my guide."

"And traipse around Europe with scores of other rubber-necking tourists during your holidays in the intense heat of July and August? No thank you. Besides, I've visited so many of these sites during my lecture circuit with **private** guides, thank you very much," he adds.

"But **I** haven't seen them, John. **I** haven't seen them. **We've** never shared these experiences. We'd see so much more than just the early Roman world. We'd have great hotels . . . and great restaurants . . . and great food and great wine . . . and lots of . . . "

"Well, if you're so determined, why don't you go on your own?"

Heartsick by his response, her only reply is, "Well . . . maybe I will."

New Day, New Pamphlet:

The amphitheater of Rome was a central component of the imperial policy of "bread and circuses," as the poet Juvenal described it. It aimed to control the citizens of Rome. But the structure itself has long outlasted the empire that built it and the reasons for its construction. It functioned almost as the city quarry, and many Renaissance buildings were later constructed using its materials.

Margot retrieves a distant memory of John's cryptic explanations upon his returns from frequent lecture tours. He would be understandably weary but underneath his fatigue was an impatience to describe in detail what she wanted to hear. She often felt a "withholding" which could have provided a thrilling commentary for both herself and, in turn, what she would have passed on to her own students.

Suddenly, Margo hears, "We love your shoes."

One of the Dutch girls has quietly walked up beside her as the group stands at the entrance to the colusseum. This startling whisper brings Margot back to the present. They are at the edge of the sand-covered portion of the colosseum's main floor with its four levels of seating rising above and around them. Most of the floor is missing, allowing them to view the lower areas of the colosseum where gladiators and wild animals were kept before ascending to the main arena. Once again she is reminded she is not entirely present.

She smiles a thank you about the shoe remark and turns back to the guide. Fleetingly, she thinks, "I must be friendlier with my group."

Previous to her departure, Margot had arrived home to find John holding the UPS delivery of her airline tickets. As she walked through the front door, he asked, "What the hell is this?"

"Well, I decided I **would** go on the tour by myself. Why not? What's standing in my way?"

"You . . . are going . . . alone . . . to Europe . . . on your own."

"But I won't **be** alone. I'm the 12th person to sign up for this early Roman excursion tour. I have a guide and I'm with the same group for 21 days. I'm really excited."

They spend the month before her departure in icy silence. Perhaps only a dozen words pass between them. They walk in parallel, she thinks, like railroad tracks. When John attends his parents' Sunday dinners on his own, Margot realizes the extent of his "deep freeze". John's mother phones Margot repeatedly trying to understand how this estrangement has suddenly occurred.

Margot finds it difficult to explain. Perhaps it began years ago when she told him of her infertility diagnosis. Perhaps it was reinforced by his frequent absences for lecture tours. Perhaps it was his reluctance to have her join him when he traveled. Whatever the reasons for this growing chasm, she has never fully anticipated the significant fall-out from signing onto this tour as a single traveler.

In retaliation to his reactions, she moves into their guest bedroom.

She stops ironing his dress shirts. The local laundry is far more capable anyway and his shirts are returned in pristine condition, wrapped and wrinkle-free. Why has she felt compelled for the past two and a half decades to spend every Monday evening chained to her ironing board?

She stops preparing his bag lunches. Cafeterias abound on his campus.

She cooks dinner only for herself and eats in front of the t.v.

When the date for her departure arrives, John has already left for an early class when she awakens. She leaves a note reminding him that this is the day she is leaving for Europe and that tonight he will return to an empty house. She also includes the date of her return. Margot taxis to the airport. She boards her plane and settles into Coach Class seating and suddenly experiences the abrupt jolt of a great loss in her life. She is genuinely excited for her forthcoming trip but needs to quash a niggling thought in the back of her mind. It keeps pushing its way forward and resists being ignored.

This is how it will feel for her now as she exercises new independent decisions.

3

SPICY TAKE-OUT

"Pretty scarf," I say, feeling the need to fill the silence.

"Vintage store. Wisdom Wednesdays. 25% off," Pauline answers.

We sit without speaking for a few moments, sipping our lattes. Once, as close friends, we had a remarkable relationship, lots of easy chatter. Twenty years later, a different story.

"Here. I want you to have it," Pauline says suddenly, untwining it from her neck.

"And if I admired your shoes?" I chuckle. "How about that cool leather jacket? If I continue with these compliments, you're ready to be left stark naked?"

"Okay, I get it," Pauline admits, laughing.

It seems her only thought is to heal our rift in any way possible. She slowly repositions her scarf and looks at me sheepishly. Again, silence.

Pauline and I live in distant cities but emailing and twice yearly visits had originally kept us close. Meeting through odd circumstances in order to share accommodation on a cruise ship, we felt instantly bonded. Both single, mid-fifties, mothers, fellow educators, we shared a similar sense of dark humor and a love of fine dining. For me, our easy relationship was like a firmly cushioned sofa: comfortable, welcoming, supportive.

Upon meeting, I should have recognized the extent of Pauline's insecure nature when she announced almost immediately that she was a Fullbright Scholar. It really meant nothing to me at the time but I would repeatedly hear her including this tidbit in conversation. Sometime during our cruise ship adventure, she discovered I also had a post-grad degree which left me feeling the first uneasy prick of her competitive nature.

Today, we are screaming along the highway in my little yellow car, delighting in a shared exuberance for a sunny day without demands. Pauline is visiting me for a long weekend and we're allowing the day to simply take us where it will.

"You are in a much better frame-of-mind since **he's** not in your life any longer," she states, breaking the silence.

This will be one of many times I will feel her critical scrutiny for my life choices. At the time it's an observation which has come out of nowhere and one I will begin to realize is her "go-to" when she wants to initiate conversation. Or, maybe demonstrate dislike. At the time, I make the mistake of assuming I can open up about this previous romantic relationship and assume she will listen sympathetically without judgment. But, over the course of our get-togethers, Pauline alludes to this man constantly, long past my painful break-up with him. I feel a strong need to tell her that I see her less and less as the confidente I once thought. However, my weak assertive nature takes over and I say nothing.

A decade into my retirement, I am fortunate to meet a lovely man who shares my passion for museums, history and traveling. It's a whirlwind romance and we are married after only six months. In the next three years we visit eight different countries in a dizzying-ly constant trek in and out of airports, arranging rental cars and occupying foreign hotels. It is a truly splendid time until he has a fatal heart attack on a Greek island. The aftermath from his death, repatriating his body, dealing with his children, working through the myriad of legalities over a two-year period in finalizing his estate, leaves me exhausted and depressed. But not once did I turn to Pauline for help. Somehow I know she is not a sympathetic ear since she offers no solace. Nor does she attend his memorial.

What saves my mental health is returning to painting. Through all of my retirement it has allowed the creative in me to emerge. I begin to paint a series of large rubenesque women and using those images, develop a card line from which I have a modicum of success. This leads me to contribute to several group shows and finally after a solid eleven months of constant painting, I am able to produce a solo show of nine large figurative pieces. Of these canvases, five are sold. I am elated. From Pauline, no encouragement, no support. She does not even attend my opening.

I continued to remain stubbornly silent from perceived slights. Like the time she states an inflammatory remark about my deceased husband: "I knew **that** about him as soon as we met. Handsome older men like him are always homophobic." Like the time she repeatedly asked, "Aren't you worried about your daughter? She's **so** thin." Like the time she visited, following the funeral, and draped herself across my bed wearing only her panties. At the time, we were preparing for sleep. Her pillow and blankets were on the couch. In that instance, I continue to floss my teeth, unable to read this odd action as anything other than an awkward come-on.

I watch her now, re-wrapping her scarf as we leave the coffee shop. She has phoned for a taxi and will soon be on her way to the ferry terminal to return to her home. Later that evening, I finally write an email explaining why I feel the growing distance between us. I have been ghosting her without an explanation. Pauline is like that highly spiced food which I initially love. But following the meal, it leaves me with severe heartburn.

She has yet to respond to my email.

4

LIFE CYCLE OF
A BUTTERFLY

"Happy, Darling?" Spencer always asks.

"As a clam," Mimi always answers and means it.

Spencer has proven to be the most perfect husband for Mimi. When their engagement is announced, Mimi's parents are only too relieved to hand Mimi's numerous peculiarities over to this sweet man. But, it seems he already knows the challenges which Mimi presents and gladly takes them on, much to her parents' chagrin.

EGG

Today is Tuesday. Mimi is in a kind of morose frame of mind. It's a mood where she occasionally allows her tendency for paranoia to run rampant, where she resurrects painful past experiences, where every single mean word, careless slight or hurtful remark from her family is located.

If Mimi begins back in 1950, she would have to start with her mother's irrational fear for her small daughter before the benefits of the polio vaccine were introduced. Mimi remembers having her little 6-year old stick legs splayed out in front of her on a bed. Her mother would then wrap them in soaking wet Hudson Bay woolen blankets believing that this questionable practice would actually thwart a deadly virus.

"Oh my gawd!" wailed Mimi's Father. "We'll be burdened with a child in braces for the rest of our lives!"

(Thanks to you, Jonas Salk. Your science persuaded my mortified father and superstitious, hysterical mother into accepting your preventative vaccine.)

Mimi has another memory, when she was perhaps nine, in which her brother is seated next to her at the dining room table. He picks up his knife and turns toward her, holding the utensil so as to obstruct his sightline. He then teases her, saying, "Mimi, you're hi-i-iding." Mimi, in tears, would bolt from the table while Mother's scolding voice would be heard above Father's shared laughter with his son.

It is around this same time that she recalls having her first twinge of what would later become widely known as "body dysmorphia". Mimi is in highschool and begins to notice how the boys stare unabashedly at the curvaceous shapes of her classmates. Sweater sets are the uniform of choice in pale pastels. Skirts were mid-calf length above bobby socks and saddle shoes. Budding breasts are positioned into cotton brassieres which result in rigid triangular shapes. Mimi craves those exact curves beneath her own pastel sweaters. Mother's solution: the falsie. Mimi, conflicted, discards this sympathetic suggestion knowing that she would feel hugely self-conscious with these sudden chest protuberances. She senses that if her own peripheral vision was alerted, so would it be for everyone else.

At this time, there is also her nose which provides additional agony. Only so much can be done with such a nose. Plastic surgery for adolescents is generally unheard of in the 60's, but Mimi throws a succession of wild tantrums resulting in her near-catatonic stupor and her parents feel it necessary to address the situation.

"Maybe she'll grow into her nose?" queries her mother.

"What? Like her giant feet?" replies her father.

Covering up the nose obsession as "the correction needed for a deviated septum", Mimi feels pleased with this final decision. And with the psychiatrist's recommendation, the plastic surgeon goes ahead with the procedure.

With the "nose" years behind her, Mimi begins to obsess about her teeth. Her brother's scathing remarks about her mouth (. . . the overbite of a racehorse) will stay with her forever. Father seems oblivious to Mimi's torment, neither offering support nor humor to cajole her from her self-pity. And so begins the many years of braces and retainers. Orthodontia is actually a pretty easy fix, Mimi discovers. Costly but effective.

Finally, it has done the trick and Mimi is set to graduate from high school as a transformed and elegant creature.

LARVA (CATERPILLAR)

Father's disapproving squint as she descends the stairs to meet her prom date underscores all her general physical dissatisfactions. Her hairstyle is an exaggerated back-combed beehive fabrication, hair sprayed into concrete. Mimi remembers kitten heels below a bouffant skirt in a swirling maze of pinks and mauve.

"You look like a giant stick of candy floss," her brother remarks. Father chuckles.

"I think you look lovely," says her date as he attaches the corsage to her wrist.

Father's hesitation in coddling his daughter's feelings stem from his own awkward ideas of parenting. He had been raised by parents who themselves felt it best for a child to "develop a thick skin". Therefore, his theories on how to raise his own children leads him to believe his remarks will "toughen 'em up" for a world which is often unkind and judgemental. In doing so, both his son and daughter have developed marked personality shortcomings: his son has become a bit of a bully and Mimi has grown to need the approval of men.

After graduating, Mimi enters the workforce and takes an office position located in the deep basement recesses of a government building housing its provincial archives. It keeps her away from society's prying eyes. It is the kind of office position for which Mimi is perfectly suited.

Anyone . . . author, historian, scholar, journalist, politician needs strict authorization in order to view the important documents and rare photographs which Mimi safeguards. Appointments are needed, requisitions required, white cotton document gloves must be worn. A separate viewing room with a clear glass partition is installed to allow Mimi unobstructed supervision of these visitors. It is the ideal job for someone like Mimi who has never felt any control in her life. Here, she controls everything.

PUPA (CHRYSALIS)

As Mimi has matured she has developed a myriad of social anxieties alongside her physical insecurities. However, working in the relative isolation of this underground office, she has been provided with the quiet solitude she has needed in order to eventually emerge.

After 20 years in this isolated working environment, Mimi begins to feel more confident in her altered appearance. She has undergone many surgical procedures over the last two decades. Since highschool, Mimi has added extensively to her rhinoplasty and orthodontia. She has had a further series of invasive surgeries: a tummy tuck, a breast augmentation, liposuction along both hips and outer thighs, a chin implant, an eyelid lift, botox into her forehead, microfibred eyebrows, removal of excess nasal labial skin, two chemical peels, collagen into her lips, fillers around her mouth and butt implants. Mimi is now 48, unmarried, still living in the basement of her parents' home and the mother of two cats.

One morning, Mimi opens her highschool newsletter announcing its 30th year reunion and is filled with a wild mix of reactions. She gives very little thought to the radical transformation of her appearance and how her newly reconstituted body will be regarded by her former classmates. For Mimi, her numerous changes have occurred over three decades and have seemed gradual. If she were to glance through her Grade XII yearbook, she would recognize her old self in a kind of detached, abstracted way. She is quite certain she now looks exactly as she has always looked, but better. Her only real audience has been her two cats and her family who have not always been sympathetic to her post-operative pain and bandages. Mimi's father, always attuned to introducing a harsher reality into her existence, reminds her that no one, not one single person from her graduating class will have any recollection of who she is as she enters the school's gymnasium for the Friday Night Meet & Greet.

"They'll look at your name tag and then up to your unrecognizable face, and then back to your name tag and then to your body and then back to your name tag. Jaws will drop."

"You kinda look like you've almost changed genders. It's that radical. Seriously, Meems," adds her brother.

Their comments are not supportive, as usual, but Mimi's main concern is to look self-assured and relaxed. She wants to appear open to reuniting with past friends and, with these thoughts in mind, carefully chooses an appropriate outfit (no cleavage).

Mimi's parents and brother wave goodbye as she backs her car out of the driveway, fully congratulating themselves on their further restraint for unsolicited comments.

ADULT

The next morning, Mimi's family is assembled at the breakfast table, eager for news.

"I can't have a meal with you," says Mimi as she enters the kitchen. "Just coffee for me. Everybody's meeting at 10:30 for brunch and then we have nine holes of golf.

My name was drawn for a foursome along with Spencer and another couple. Remember Spencer? . . . from my graduation dance?"

"You mean . . . Prom-Boy?" her startled brother asks. "You've reconnected with Prom-Boy after all these years? What did he say when he first saw you . . . and how did he EVEN recognize you?"

"Well, he seemed to know perfectly well who I was when he walked up behind me. He spoke my name as he tapped me on the shoulder. When I turned around, he looked into my eyes for a very long time and finally said . . . *"You haven't changed one bit."* And then he added . . . *"Mimi . . . you've always been a babe."*

"I'll never forget it," she adds dreamily, stirring cream into her coffee. "His exact words. Isn't that something? . . . isn't that JUST something? . . . been divorced for about five years, no kids. He looks pretty much the same. Still kinda chubby, almost bald now, sticky-out ears, beautiful eyes . . . sorry, gotta go."

As Mimi leaves the house, her family remains seated at the breakfast table, staring blankly into the space that separates them. They had only been prepared to hear tales of disappointment. They were quite unprepared for Mimi's sudden social success and re-emergence into the real world.

"Why is it we always withhold?" Mother suddenly muses, breaking the lengthy silence.

"Whatever are you talking about?" asks Mimi's brother.

". . . never been healthy to reinforce Mimi's inadequacies about appearance," Father contributes. "We've been wise over the years to avoid touching on "looks" as worthy of serious discussion despite her constant preoccupation. Even through ALL her procedures, we refrained. A child should grow up focussing on . . . other things . . . what's important in life."

"Maybe we missed opportunities to let her know her feelings were something worthy of discussion," Mother continues. "We've withheld. Simple as that. And now she turns to the welcoming voice which really hears her."

"She **IS** a real looker now," Father concedes. After another lengthy silence, he adds, "What do you suppose she sees in him?"

"Perhaps, he just treats her really, really well," replies Mother.

Six months after their honeymoon, Mimi and her new husband are driving home from a night out.

"Feelin' peachy, Darling?" Spencer inquires.

"Keen," Mimi responds with a smile, and means it.

5

ABSURDIST PHILOSOPHY

PROLOGUE:

Walter has always subscribed to the theory that, as adults, we partner with people who caused us the most uncomfortable childhood challenges. Some psychologists believe we continually search out those people in order to finally assert ourselves. Reflecting on his own situation, Walter realizes he has probably married his father. And today, it is like being reunited with himself as a long ago friend, someone with whom he'd lost all contact.

Walter had originally only intended to audit this philosophy class but when Elizabeth makes her usual grimace at the mention of his intentions, his purpose gathers steam. In his hand he still holds the pamphlet advertising the evening offerings for Adult Learners: **The**

Absurdist Philosophy of Albert Camus Tuesday night 6:30 - 9:30, reads the announcement.

Walter could imagine himself walking across the campus to his assigned building and climbing the stairs to his assigned classroom. He would have parked his car in a nearby lot, gathered together his newly purchased school supplies and set off, walking across the quad with the excitement of a first-grader.

Elizabeth, on hearing his news, slowly lays her fruit peeler onto the counter, pursing her lips in that way she does when forced to make yet another intrusive decision.

"Audit? Like pay full price but receive no credit? Let's just slow down and rethink this idea, WallyBoy. First of all . . . . . . "

But Walter has already blocked her advice. He has long ago discovered a technique in their third decade of marriage which he can easily resurrect when needed. Her intolerable words become drowned out in a kind of high frequency head-squeal he can self-induce. It is like an inner ear tinnitus which he can actually summon at will. He remembers the first time he was able to block what he called "Elizabeth-Noise". She was again telling one of her personal stories which held her audience spellbound. He had to admit she WAS greatly entertaining. Except for the fact that he had heard this exact story, verbatim, how many countless times, over how many years? As his eyes begin to glaze over, he realizes he can still see her lips moving but her words are being swallowed up by the high-pitched whining. He likens it to a wind tunnel.

". . . the advantage of which completely eludes me." Elizabeth offers in summation.

She had been peeling apples and pears when he entered the kitchen. She's making her customary jellies, jams, compotes and sauces. She has purchased flat after flat of seasonal fruit, pectin, sugar, mason jars, lids and sealing rings along with needed supplies for label-making and begins this yearly task with the kind of driven energy needed for launching a military bivouac. She carries an agenda in her head known only to herself and relinquishes all domestic responsibility until each jam task is completed. She hardly eats or sleeps until every combination of fruits gives way to row after row of various-sized jars, assembled, labeled and arranged on the many shelves (built by Walter) to hold the fruits of her labors. When the jam undertaking is completed, she's ready to launch the cucumbers, beans, carrots, cabbage and corn for pickling over winter. This parade of preservation is only completed in time to begin the antipasto-making at the beginning of December, just in time for Christmas.

Such has been their September-December routine for 50 years except for July 1999 when they both came down with a serious bronchial infection, October 2009 when they took a Mediterranean cruise and August 2010 when Elizabeth broke an ankle. Their lives are ordered and consistently regulated with a precision that is both admired and mocked.

Elizabeth has grown into a woman with many compulsions, one of which is the perception that she must always appear incredibly busy. She needs to be perceived as having the highest of work ethics. Hence, her need to keep Walter on the same gerbil wheel right alongside herself. She likes to answer the phone in a breathless state like she has just run up several flights of stairs. In all likelihood, she has simply just strode the length of her kitchen linoleum after wiping crumbs off a counter.

"I have a system, and from it, I will not deviate" needs to be stitched onto a sampler and hung over their fireplace mantle, thinks Walter. The mantra ". . . neither wind nor rain nor driving sleet . . ." of the U.S. postal service rings true.

"This night class is my chance to study absurdist philosophy which simply appeals to me at the moment," Walter responds flatly. "My only other extra-curricular is Wednesday golf. Otherwise, I am ALWAYS . . . ALWAYS commandeered to follow YOUR agenda, Elizabeth."

Wednesday golf had become his most coveted day. Walter is an average golfer, more interested in the goofy shared jocularity of guy-time than any need to improve his game. Lowering his handicap is the farthest thing from his mind. Walking 18 holes, rain or shine, and their customary post-game "accounting" affords him the kind of light-hearted banter he craves. It is a release from the demands of "E-lizard-breath" and her endless to-do lists.

His golf buddies have been a consistent foursome for three decades. They each have their niche placement within the group: There's Andy . . . compulsive talker, failing eyesight due to macular degeneration, general bon vivant; everybody's best bud, gourmet cook. Then there's Bill . . . , sphinx-like silent between hearty horse laughs, generous, giving, showing possible signs of early cognitive decline. Tommy . . . sneaky but loveable golf cheat, loyal, profane, overweight . . . and finally, Walter: quietly humorous, constant seeker-of-the-hilarious, patient, supportive, unflinchingly kind.

They have their post-game 19th hole rituals which involves whiskey shots and the settling-up of who owes whom and how much. Walter, the group's accountant, has tallied the 25 cents per infraction and/or win/loss for each hole for each of the foursome. They use decidedly non-golf references for every fault and take enormous delight in holding each other accountable. Over the years their words for "slice", "shank", "in the weeds", "gimme's" etc. have resulted in the craziest, most nonsensical terms, which provides them endless delight. It's their grown-up version of a secret playground hand shake. An exclusive club---outsiders not allowed.

This particular conversation with Elizabeth about his choice of evening class sparks a sudden-and--not-so-quiet explosion inside Walter's head. He takes note of the startled look on her face as her eyes widen in surprise. He senses his voice quavering along with what he feels is his face suddenly reddening. His chest is tightening and he doesn't know where to direct his eyes.

Dammit, he curses to himself. Crap . . . Am I welling up? No, . . . No . . . No . . . Not now. Lordy, don't let me cry.

"DAMMIT, ELIZABETH . . . ENOUGH! E-BLOODY-NUFF!!" he shouts, filled with a sudden rage. And in a cascade of random and disjointed mumblings, he blurts out a stream of largely disconnected words which have no meaning.

"Easy, Wal-Wal, e-a-sy. Come sit down. Let's t-a-a-ke a breath. You need to calm yourself."

He hears her patronizing tone as additional gasoline on the fire and feels a disrespect for his feelings. They move to the living room where they sit across from each other, separated by the coffee table.

"What DO you mean, Walter. **MY** agenda? Pl-ea-s-e elaborate,"

He ignores the sneer in her voice and knows the conversation will soon begin to veer dangerously off-course. He clears his throat.

"Elizabeth, in all fairness to both of us, we're not the people we originally married."

"I'm waiting, Walter."

"We've developed certain patterns over our many years."

"My agenda, Walter, Remember?"

"I'm getting there, Elizabeth. Please let me . . . my own pace."

"Walter . . . I have apples on the---"

"SHUT UP, SHUT UP, SHUT UP, SHUT UP, SHUT UP, SHUT UP, SHUT UP," he shouts. "PLEASE . . . SHUT . . . UP!".

Hardly ever, over the length of their entire marriage, has either of them used offensive words with each other. Certainly no profanities. In fact, Elizabeth has frequently mentioned to her quilting circles that her lengthy marriage is partially due to their avoidance of any and all harsh or nasty words. Rather, it seems they have chosen the deadlier alternative: silence.

But in her head she knows what Walter is driving at. Over their years together, Elizabeth HAS definitely noticed Walter's growing overly compliant nature towards her wishes. She knows she drives the boat. She knows her agenda dominates. She knows all this and more. She realizes his silent behaviors have resulted largely because of her dominance.

But, Elizabeth still likes to present a unified front. When in social situations, she is often cloyingly attentive to his needs. If asked a question, no matter how trivial, she will often defer her answer by first asking Walter for his input. Walter, at this point, is usually "in the wind tunnel" and only realizes his opinion is required when all eyes turn toward him. In fashioning his response, he is often tempted to reply, "what she said" but realizes he'd later end up paying for that little bit of flippancy with her prolonged silent treatment.

"I've lost my voice," he states suddenly after a lengthy silence.

"Say what?" she inquires, "You've lost your voice? What AM I hearing?" This is followed by the dramatic gesture of raising both her arms and looking about for assistance from a heavenly source.

"That's enough, Elizabeth. You KNOW full well what I'm talking about."

"And what does THAT have to do with what you call my agenda?"

Elizabeth, of course, DOES know exactly what he's talking about but being a bit of the bully that she is, her twisted delight in his discomfort takes over.

It is at this point that Walter, out of sheer frustration, begins to weep. Large tears streak his silent face. He sits mute amidst this copious cascade, unwilling to be embarrassed or to rush for a tissue. Elizabeth is startled from her superior thoughts. She stares transfixed at his sudden breakdown, feeling an enormous wave of shame wash over her entire body. She has pushed him over the edge. She alone has done this. When has he ever cried in front of her? And, in an odd "come to Jesus" moment, both Walter and Elizabeth know they stand before each other completely naked. It is that moment in a marriage which leads either to resurrection . . . or the shitter. They sit in total silence. Elizabeth stares at Walter's tears which continue to stream unchecked.

And then, in a complete non-sequitur of total inspiration, Elizabeth suddenly says, "Walter . . . tell me about absurdist philosophy. Tell me about Albert Camus."

Walter opens his eyes, sensing a trap, unsure of the olive branch being extended. He stares into Elizabeth's face. There is no smirky "stink-eye" visible. Her brimming eyes hold only sympathy. He maintains his gaze intently and now watches as Elizabeth allows her own tears to fall unchecked.

He hesitates to break this tender spell, being reminded of their mutual vulnerability, fifty years ago when they were newly in love.

"Elizabeth . . . why don't you go to the stove and turn off the fruit. Come back and sit here . . . beside me, . . . so we can talk . . . and I'll tell you what I know about Albert Camus and his absurdist philosophy."

6

CORDELIA

As one of the widows of a fallen British soldier from the Third Anglo-Afghan War, she sits with head bowed, contemplating her nervous fingers twisting a crumpled handkerchief. The cannon salutes thunder, causing all to flinch with every boom. A custom hardly meant to console the mourners, she thinks. Another show of military might in the face of unaccountable loss. Children robbed of fathers. Wives robbed of husbands.

"What sense of purpose drives you to fight for the imperial rights of Britain in another far-off country, for god's sake?" Cordelia remembered imploring her husband after his return from the battlefields of France in The Great War. "How far afield are you compelled to travel once again to serve the crown?"

"I'm a soldier. That is my calling. How can you even question my purpose?"

Cordelia's husband had always been described as . . . "a soldier, right down to his socks." His father and grandfather, his great grandfather and even his great-great, had all served in Britain's military. His father had fought at Sevastopol in the Crimea, his grandfather at Mysore in the Indian conflict, his great grand-pappa had been at Waterloo and his great-great at Trafalgar. Photos on mantles proudly attest to the efforts of Cordelia's husband's line. In each, below waxed mustaches and stiff-collared jackets, their chests are ablaze with ribbons and medals.

As she dusts them, Cordelia gazes at these ornately framed photos and wonder why it was they were so driven to serve. This direction seemed to have been predetermined, even with her husband, from infancy. When questioned about his childhood, he always recalled his toys as swords or scabbards or helmets pilfered from conflicts. Games, he said, were continuously centered around destroy and conquer. These dictates had been set in stone long before she had ever been considered as his wife. The British mindset understood that no greater training could exist for a privately schooled young man, coming of age, than to have his military involvement coupled with a few years at an upper level university. After that, his diplomatic position was secured. The houses of parliament were filled with such men. They had all evolved out of the same system.

Cordelia's husband's direction had continued in the military. He had risen through the ranks quickly. Now his body occupies a flag-draped casket.

Cordelia was born at the turn of the 20th century, the end of the Victorian era. She had been raised by indulgent and loving parents who wanted nothing more than a happy young bride, betrothed to a well-established and prosperous suitor.

She had no unpleasant memories from her childhood other than having her long hair painfully brushed free of tangles. She lovingly remembers being hoisted into the air by her father, followed by the raspy feeling of his beard as he hugged her. She had clear memories of tea parties with her wonderful Uncle George at which they would both wear Mommy's cast-off hats and kimonos and pretend to gossip.

She never questioned when told that her immediate goal, after her privately tutored education in Greek mythology, needlepoint and piano lessons, was to gather an elaborate trousseau, replete with extensive household linens. Additionally, she was to assemble suitable undergarments, corsets, underslips, petticoats, sleeping apparel etc., to enter into her imminent marriage. This was to be the direction of her life. These items were pressed, folded and stowed into the deep recesses of the elaborately carved walnut chest presented to her from her beloved Uncle George.

"A good marriage is the only way a woman can secure her future": an aphorism now brought to mind as she looks about at the other widows at this memorial service. All are in black as she is. She feels sadness, of course, but more clearly, Cordelia quietly realizes her husband's death affords her a newly-found independence which is currently enhanced by the British government's recently instituted pension measures for widows and orphans.

Twelve years ago, as a betrothed woman, thrilled beyond description with the fairytale wedding she was planning and the life she would soon live with her new husband, she had not foreseen his "incendiary" nature. In the short time she had known him, she considered him to be a conscientious man of quiet reflection, much like her adored father and wonderful Uncle George.

Gradually, over the decade of her marriage, she has observed his unwavering and rigid military bearing. It seems to deny him the ability to appreciate a jovial situation. He looks suspiciously upon all humor. His short respites between military campaigns trigger his need to assert strict authority over home and hearth. It is with a certain loathing that Cordelia begins to dread his returns from war zones. She also feels resentment at being robbed of the solitary pleasures she enjoys when he is gone.

She had learned early on that her husband views her efforts as frivolous and unbecoming. She should be content, he said, to maintain the home and not be off roaming the hills wearing wild assortments of clothing and appearing generally unkempt. Who exactly, she wonders, was informing him of these behaviours?

"I've buried two parents over the past decade," Cordelia shouts at him. "Both times when you were gone on campaigns. I've had no one close for support, other than our local vicar and wonderful Uncle George."

Both deaths were extremely difficult for Cordelia. Uncle George's seat in the government meant he was obligated to return to London shortly after each funeral. It was always with a heavy heart that she'd wave him off.

"After Mother's funeral, he invited me to London for a change of scenery so I could tour the galleries and see the shops."

"Your mother's younger brother is hardly the social connection I wish for you, Cordelia. Where are your own friends? Where are the wives of my military comrades? Why aren't you hosting afternoon tea with the other ladies? It's unseemly for you to be tramping through the forests unaccompanied. And it's equally unseemly to be associated with George's sort of . . . of . . . London crowd as a married woman. Your Uncle George is not the proper influence I can encourage. Don't you women still host "at homes"?

Hearing this, Cordelia slowly shakes her head and rolls her eyes. As she exits the parlor, she continues to hear him mumble . . . "can't believe such a gentle custom as the "at-home" is no longer observed . . . social obligations need to be fulfilled . . ."

He wasn't completely wrong about her lack of female friends. She had been raised as an only child and had no immediate cousins nearby. Her parents and Uncle George had been her willing substitutes for playmates. Growing up, Cordelia never gave much thought to her lifestyle. She had a vivid imagination and was frequently described by her nannies as "living entirely in her own head". Every hired tutor reported she was a self-motivated student who knew how to entertain herself. Cordelia had never, in the nineteen years before her wedding, experienced boredom . . . until the ten years following her marriage.

And now, widowed at age 29 and childless, Cordelia stands amongst the throngs of other sad women, accepting the gratitude of the British government for her husband's military contributions.

Having been unable to conceive, Cordelia's essential role has been thwarted. Instead, she now takes great solace in setting up her easel on steep hillsides and returns home, hours later, wearing a huge smile and paint splattered garments. Her cook and gardener assess her disarray with patient humour and share sideways glances. Despite these gentle scoldings, Cordelia is grateful for her release from the monotonous repetition of running a household. It seems that her cook could fill that capacity quite well. Perhaps, she occasionally ponders, with everything considered, she may not have been well suited for motherhood.

During her marriage, Cordelia didn't question her infertility. Rather, she felt the doctor's description of her "inhospitable womb" as her own unconscious rejection of her husband's less-than-impassioned sexual appetites. She had voraciously read all the current novels of desire and romance. Austen, Elliott, Sand, James and Hardy are among latent Victorian era favorites. They detail the male and his romantic pursuits in explicit terms. Cordelia's husband did not seem driven by normal male appetites. Did she desire a rutting beast? Certainly not. What Cordelia desired was a man who spoke to her heart.

She had made sure to carefully hide those books from her husband's prying eyes upon his returns. Thackeray's novel, <u>Vanity Fair,</u> became largely responsible for awakening in her an awareness of women and their journeys navigating male oppression as well as the class system. She grew noticeably restless with these nagging thoughts and once, upon his return from a deployment along the western front, began a conversation about the suppression of women. It ended when she was stiffly informed of his concerns for her mental health.

"Great advances in gynecology are being made," he informed Cordelia, "in the "repositioning" of the female organs to control hysterical behaviour." He leaves her with this shocking pronouncement before departing once again, this last time for Afghanistan. Against her opposition, he says he will be forced to make decisions for her hospitalization upon his return. But, as fate would have it, he is soon dead from injuries sustained during a border skirmish.

"Such odd circumstances have prevailed in allowing me to keep my body intact."

She had reported this bittersweet news to Uncle George as they followed the coffin to the cemetery.

Two years later Codelia leaves her village home and gardens in the care of her domestic staff, Clara and Thomas, and emerges into London's social scene under the tutelage of Uncle George. As she familiarizes herself with his fashionable High Street Kensington home and his equally fashionable friends, she comes to realize her own naivete in the years prior to her arrival in London. Previously, she had been far removed from London in the small village of Twickenham. It had ideally suited her husband's sense of "large fish in a small pond" but for Cordelia, she knows it kept her isolated and dependent.

Increasingly, she realizes two things:

1. She had unwittingly played her part in a marriage which had slowly proven a disappointment. If she were to describe their physical attraction she would think of it as hesitant and polite. It hadn't been a completely loveless union, but still, it had left her feeling largely unfulfilled. He was frequently fatigued, an excuse which filled her with quiet contempt. It remained for her to initiate their lovemaking which made her feel uncomfortably dominant. He had also grown more wordless during their decade of marriage; his returns from war were followed by long bouts of solitary isolation in his office. He had never been given to easy conversation under any circumstance, but now days would pass with hardly more than a dozen sentences spoken between them. Even in his intense moments of intimate passion, he seemed devoid of heartfelt expression.

2. She isn't the model of domesticity which she assumed would magically reveal itself in her as a married woman. She has patterned her expectations on her parents' behaviours. She views what they had modeled as exactly what would develop in her by . . . simply wanting it to be so.

Cordelia has found her grief immediately relieved by her London stay in Uncle George's pied-a-terre. She has arrived for the season and knows she can experience life without censure. It is thrilling to be his hostess. His dinner parties have become the occasions most coveted by cultural London. Uncle George is a member of the House of Commons and holds great sway as an orator and, at his dinner parties, is a compelling raconteur.

His dinners are frequented by the most controversial figures of science, politics and the arts. They now provide Uncle George with the opportunity to present his niece to a group of stimulating acquaintances far from the quaint and provincial lifestyle she has previously experienced. He regularly welcomes an exciting array of dinner guests: jockeys from Ascot, the adventurous Amelia Earhardt, actress Sarah Berhardt, noted psychiatrist Sigmund Freud, literary wit Noel Coward, dancer Josephine Baker and into this milieu . . . Cordelia, very much the neophyte.

The twentieth century has brought about the emergence of evolving economies and social structures. Fashions are changing, industry is changing and in the wake of the Great War, the defining characteristics of the role of women are changing. At Uncle George's dinners, the group which Cordelia finds most intriguing are the high-level courtesans and mistresses who have accompanied many of Uncle George's fellow politicians. These women are not shy about sharing the secrets of their extravagant lifestyles, fine food and beautiful clothes. Cordelia finds them to be sharp business women of strong intellect. She is impressed with those who understand the inevitable fading of their beauty and the importance of investing in a future.

In the midst of Cordelia's intellectual awakening, Uncle George recognizes her vulnerability. So, it is with great care that he is cautious regarding her interactions with those who attend his dinners. Meeting D.H., as Uncle George has always referred to him, is a moment of immense impact for Cordelia. She remembers the exact colour of the curtains which framed his face when she first met his eyes. The late afternoon sun was shining through those curtains creating a halo effect around his head. It took place in Uncle George's kitchen and Cordelia had descended to the lower floor in order to oversee dinner preparations. D.H. had also arrived into the kitchen, perhaps to cause mischief . . . et voila.

D.H. was an acknowledged author drawn to the personal stories of the people he met. For such a writer, Cordelia's life represented every aspect of the lingering Victorian repression of women. She did not find him particularly attractive but his penetrating gaze held her attention completely. Never having had the total focus of a man outside of her papa and Uncle George, Cordelia finds herself revealing her deepest needs and thoughts to D.H. in a wild rush of words. She is entirely captivated by his intense interest in her.

Their affair is brief but completely consuming for Cordelia. She has craved the reciprocation of intense passion and feels in her bones that he adores her. Despite Uncle George's objections, they closet themselves in a romantic little Bournemouth cottage by the sea and for three weeks live a fantasy. It ends one morning with a sharp knock on the cottage door and a note delivered following their morning tea. It seems, at his wife's insistance, that D.H. needs to return immediately to his writing in order to fulfill contractual obligations for the novel he has so abruptly abandoned.

"You have . . . a wife," Cordelia states flatly, staring in disbelief at the publisher's note.

"Yes, I do. And she is entirely accepting of my short-term dalliances."

"Well, haven't I been a first-class fool. I never thought to inquire about a wife, or, of this as just a dalliance."

And so their conversation continues along this line for the next thirty minutes. D.H. is given to supplying the most facile and glib excuses for his philandering. She is as disgusted with his rationale concerning extramarital affairs as her own gullibility.

Cordelia takes a separate train back to London. Uncle George meets her at Piccadilly, feeling completely responsible for D.H.'s deceit.

"You knew about his wife, Uncle George?"

"Yes." he confesses. "D.H. assured me that he had informed you. I should not have accepted him at his word. He has wounded you deeply."

Together they walk to his townhouse on Allen Street. He urges her to stay with him for the remainder of the season but she feels it necessary to return to Twickenham in order to come to terms with events of this past month.

The next night over dinner, Cordelia sits with her sympathetic cook and gardener. She fully reveals her heady infatuation with D.H. followed by her crashing disappointment. "Shan't make that mistake again," she quietly mutters to them. Clara and Thomas share a look, hoping the likelihood for such folly is not possible.

Over the next four months, her long forays into the forest and open hillsides help to ease her sense of discontent. En plein air painting is an easy calling for Cordelia. She has always been pleased with her investment in a portable easel which allows her to set up her painting equipment outdoors. Oil tubes, brushes, turpentine and rags are packed into a rucksack which comfortably straps to her back. It combines the two activities she loves the most. Today, in mid brush stroke, while working on a pastoral scene, she finds herself overcome with a wild surge of frustration. Using her largest brush, she begins slashing paint onto her canvas with whatever colors still remain on her palette. It feels enormously rewarding to give vent to these feelings. It's like she's plumbing the depths of her own interior landscape.

Uncle George's visit is entirely unexpected. Cordelia's cook points him in the right direction and he follows a worn path through the woods until it opens onto a series of rolling hillsides where he eventually finds her. Cordelia has set up her easel under the canopy of a huge tree and is wildly flinging paint onto what he observes might be a self-portrait. Several more empty canvases lean against the tree trunk.

As he walks up behind her, he chides, "Only one reply in over four months. Is that any way to treat your favorite uncle?"

"I'm sorry, George. I've been so distracted . . . and preoccupied."

And with that, Cordelia slowly turns to face him, removing her paint-smattered smock to reveal the beginnings of her swollen pregnant stomach.

Over the next four months, Cordelia's daily forays into the forest have resulted in a new and aggressive painting style. Layered onto portraits of George, Clara, Thomas and herself, arbitrary colors are used for skin tones and hair. Variations of these portraits are made up of oranges and greens and are combined with the boldness of mustard yellow and fuschia. Cordelia's landscapes use purples and reds for foliage, tree trunks are blue. Colours straight from the tube provide the most vivid effect.

Clara, Thomas and Uncle George are only too happy to sit while she quickly charcoals their poses onto canvas. Thomas' gardening shed has become the needed additional storage for art supplies. She has stockpiled enough oil paint and brushes for the several remaining months of her pregnancy and works with feverish intensity before her baby arrives.

Oddly, over the course of her confinement, Cordelia has avoided thinking of her condition and what has led to this situation. Aside from her baby's kicks and occasional hiccoughs, she is only made aware of her increasingly large and unwieldy size when Clara and Thomas help her set up her equipment. Frequent stops along her familiar forest trails are needed. Today, her back aches, her feet ache, her stamina is flagging.

When Cordelia's water breaks in the middle of the following night, it's up to Clara and Thomas to assist with the delivery. While Cordelia's isolation has undoubtedly protected her and her household from the devastation of the Spanish flu, it has also rendered every doctor or midwife unavailable for home deliveries. Nonetheless, into this chaos, Cordelia gives birth to a sweet baby girl whom she names Grace.

Motherhood for Cordelia is a profound experience. She has fallen in love with her child. Clara and Thomas are the additional doting adults who become happy, gibbering, foolish clowns continuously trying to elicit smiles from Cordelia's baby. Tiny Grace is the center of the universe for all involved.

London is now just starting to emerge from the devastating spread of the post-war pandemic. It is at this point that Uncle George arrives after having been quarantined in his London home for the first twelve months of Grace's life.

"She is the perfect angel you have so aptly described," he says, gazing wistfully into Grace's crib. I am so pleased for you. And now the three of us will form the tightest bond. I have great plans for my little grand niece . . . I also have further news, Cordelia . . . it's about D.H."

"George, under no conditions is he ever to know that he is Grace's father."

"And he never shall. So put your mind at rest. No, it's not that . . . D.H. has just had his new book published. It's called *Lady Chatterley's Lover*. It's written from the perspective of a groundskeeper who is employed by a man of high status. The central heroine's life bares a striking resemblance to yours but I don't think any of it will connect to you. I thought you should know."

"So, you've read it?"

"Yes, and it's quite steamy. I know I told him intimate details. You may find he has quoted your words almost verbatim. I have a copy for you. I'm sorry, Cordelia. I know this is painful."

Over the next two days, as she reads her exact comments coming back to her off the page, she thinks Uncle George is right. It's like D.H. has remembered every word.

"He has left me naked. I am stripped bare."

As the next three years pass, Cordelia continues to live a quiet country life. By the time she celebrates Grace's third birthday, she has amassed a considerable number of canvases and is approaching London galleries for representation. She has continued to paint in an abstract style combining the brutally vivid colours of Fauvism and the raw feelings of Expressionism. Uncle George wants to intercede in order for her presence as a female artist to have the full attention of the galleries. Her paintings are signed only as C. Boothe, and reveal the powerful presence of the naked human form amidst foliage and forest. Her opening show is entitled "From The Garden" and suggests Eden. It illustrates the evolution of man and woman into what has emerged post war.

One day, following the opening of her showing, Cordelia spots a familiar face entering the gallery which is displaying her solo exhibition. D.H. and his wife are looking for avant garde art, they say, to decorate their salon. She overhears them as they speak to the gallery owner, "We are looking for something shocking and extraordinary . . . something which moves us."

Cordelia has coincidentally arrived with a new canvas and just happens to be on-site in a back room.

As D.H. scans the walls, he comments, "What forceful, strong work. Who is this artist?"

"Perhaps you would like to meet the creator? Let me introduce you," the gallery owner suggests.

When Cordelia emerges from the back room, it is not D.H.'s face, with mouth agape, which we observe. It is Cordelia's face which reveals the shock of his complete lack of recognition when they meet. It takes her several seconds to realize he has absolutely no immediate recollection of her.

"I am amazed that these paintings have been created by a woman," D.H. states, staring at Cordelia's face . . . "extraordinary . . . I feel we have previously met. Is that possible?"

After several uncomfortable moments in which no one speaks, his wife says to Cordelia, "We are very impressed with your work." She then turns to her husband and adds, "Aren't we, my dear?"

Further pleasantries are exchanged after which Cordelia wills herself to leave the gallery. Any further dealings will be handled by the gallery owner. She walks to her underground stop, resisting the urge to glance back. Cordelia reminds herself of the numerous times she has wondered how such a chance encounter with D.H. would unfold. How many times had she stood in front of her bathroom mirror practicing the words she would use to reduce him to ashes? On impulse, she enters a tea shop to sit quietly for a moment.

It's a dreary little tea room with the kind of cloyingly sentimental wallpaper she detests. She places her order and now sits quietly staring at her empty cup and saucer while the tea steeps. She realizes she is no longer filled with the rage of rejection. She feels neither remorse nor mortification. Instead, she is aware of a certain release from something unnamed which has held her captive for the last four years.

7

LILLIAN THROUGHOUT

This is a short story about a long life. It's about some of the men involved with a particular woman over the course of her 80 years. I'm sorry the men don't figure more importantly even though the stories they tell are theirs. But this narrative is more about Lillian and her serially monogamous life.

JAY:

It was Lillian who always agitated for us to move to the west coast with its wondrous mountains and ocean. She longed to live in a place which honored its heritage and architecture. So we settled into a beautiful ocean-front city which showcased an inner harbor which once featured a turn-of-the-century Hudson Bay fort. That fact alone delighted her to no end. She was equally thrilled when she found the heritage tile markers embedded in a sidewalk location indicating the HBC's northwest bastion.

Lillian and I had grown up in Saskatoon and leaving the prairies was harder for me than her. I was leaving professional opportunities as well as friends and family. For Lillian, it provided an immense release from sub-zero wind-chill winters and summer mosquitoes. She loved the sweeping prairie landscapes, I know, but longed for a more varied topography.

CHUCK:
I had delivered Lillian's baby Annie the previous year so our relationship was as doctor-patient. When Lillian and her husband sought counseling for their growing estrangement after their baby was born, they not only sought me out to assist with their communication problems but, oddly enough, ended up purchasing an old stone coach house within half a block of mine unbeknownst to either of us at the time. Even though the house purchase was a surprise, our eventual union seemed inevitable.

Our time together was short and rather volcanic. I was not the father figure Lillian wanted for her child. I already had two pre-adolescent girls and a furious ex-wife who presented an unsavory challenge for Lillian.

TOM:
I met Lillian through friends when she had been on her own for two years raising her 3-year old daughter, Annie. Oddly enough, little Annie resembled me with her curly blond hair and chubby red cheeks. I was instantly the dad whom Lillian wanted for Annie. I created giant human habitrails out of cardboard boxes, brought home a kitten, cooked endless mountains of pancakes, and played board games. We bought a house, hung wallpaper, planted a Christmas tree hedge and were beginning to teach Annie

to ride a bike. We were a family. We traveled to Holland for six weeks one summer and rode bicycles along magical canals.

DEWAYNE:

I met Lillian in a massive art studio setting which she shared with 12 other undergrad students on the university campus. I think she was taken with me because I was a tradesman. I was someone who could build or fix anything. She had been on her own for several years, raising her daughter, Annie, who was now in middle school. She seemed comfortable with all of life's prospects. She had friends and community and told me she loved being the single side-kick to her married couple friends. She was unencumbered with a marriage and could set her own agenda.

Together we found a great fixer-upper on an inland arm of the ocean and set out to landscape the garden, add an addition and restore the interior to its 1911 style. It was Lillian who held the credentials for mortgaging and the needed refinancing. This became a constant source of friction for us as well as the fact that her monthly teaching salary far outstripped anything I could supply. The imbalance of power began to cause a disquiet for us and soon other irritations surfaced. Lillian discovered I had abandoned an infant daughter years before I met her. This became an issue for us after my daughter was the one who made contact and Lillian slowly realized I was an abandoner.

I was not a well-read man. Lillian's life, as well as the friends with whom we associated, were largely involved in the academic world. I was proving myself to be woefully unscholarly in Lillian's eyes. I once overheard her describe the angers which surface in very short men and knew she referenced me.

When she discovered I was having an affair, she offered me $5000 in order to motivate my departure. I wanted to stay on, living in her house but that money was my "out". I was gone in a shot, cashed her cheque within an hour, leaving her with a large mortgage to service. But, somehow, Lillian found substantial financing for continuing all the needed renovations. It enraged me to realize she had located enough financial support. Once again I felt cheated so I sneaked back onto her property one morning (after I knew she had gone to school) and took back my cement mixer.

ROD:

I moved into Lillian's small backyard cottage for about eight months. It had been fashioned out of an old neglected garage. Lillian had enlisted the help of her carpenter friend Rocky to build this little house after Dewayne had vacated the property. I was one of her first renters.

I misread her signals, I guess. I thought she was interested in me romantically, as someone more than just a tenant, and hoped she was receptive to a relationship. When I made a move, she let me know immediately that she wasn't available. So I retaliated by searching through city records to find evidence of her application for building permits. Finding none, I confronted her with my discovery. I could see I "had her" from the look on her face.

Lillian said I displayed possessive behaviours and resented my pursuit by blackmailing her emotions. She ended my rental lease when she said I also demonstrated signs of stalking. Besides, she said, her daughter Annie was moving back to the island and needed housing while returning for post secondary studies. Lillian reminded me strongly of how my ex-wife had behaved before we divorced.

NEAL:
I had just been diagnosed as clinically depressed and was being medicated for unpredictable manic behaviours with wild mood swings and episodes of flagrant over-spending. I met Lillian through a ballroom dancing club. She bought one of my ocean-going kayaks because I was broke. She also bought me a microwave before sending me on my way.

RUDY:
I was very proud of my extensive properties and in particular my spacious cliff-top house above the ocean in Sooke. As a wealthy, retired (Austrian) gentleman, I had built a beautiful house with an indoor pool, sauna and ozonated whirlpool to rival any retreat oasis anywhere. Lillian told me she felt suspicious and uncomfortable with my extensive collection of medieval, Italian, religious artifacts which she felt could only have come into my possession through inherited Nazi lootings.

FRANK;
I met Lillian on the Dallas Road walkway overlooking the ocean at Ogden Point on a particularly windy afternoon.

A sudden gust blew my hat off and from the look on Lillian's face, I knew I needed to rethink my comb-over.

BUTCH;

I was a highschool athletics teacher and met Lillian through mutual friends. I think she found me to be a nice enough fellow, but, as she described to a friend, not a compelling brain trust.

SAM:

I was the father of a highly disabled adult son. I know I was a kind man but one who presented numerous encumbrances for Lillian. She seemed to dislike my strenuous vegan diet coupled with my unusually high consumption of coca-cola.

ROLAND:

I met Lillian at a fitness club. Over the course of several dates, I revealed to her that I had left Ontario after being released from incarceration for drug trafficking. I had just been forced to pawn my beautiful Oyster watch to finance, among other things, another month of health club membership. I appreciated her gesture to go dutch for coffee or drinks but sensed my time with her was short-lived.

HANK:

I've always been described as tall. And as an afterthought, tall and arrogant. Even my hair I have heard is described as arrogant. I felt, at first, Lillian mistook all this as confidence but soon realized I was friendless for good reason. I know I presented well but hidden underneath were many decades of narcissism and sociopathy. I had left a marriage and two adult children, moved across the country after several years as a Toronto firefighter, to reside in a camper-trailer as part of my so-called vagabond retirement plan.

My time with Lillian ended abruptly when she announced, "I've had enough." Tired of my unpredictable tirades, tired of my frustrations with my own declining left-ear hearing loss, tired of my penny-pinching, checks-and-balances financial tallying, tired of my conversational manipulations, tired of my unpredictable moody withdrawals . . . she was just plain tired. So what if I once pinched her nipple to wake her up from a deep sleep?

WILLIAM:

I laughed when Lillian told me that our meeting (through a dating website) was like a window opening into a stuffy, stagnant, humid room.

We met at a great little coffee house in Old Town. We had mutual friends, both being retired from the same school district. I had been an administrator and Lillian a classroom teacher. We had crossed teaching paths frequently but had no distinct memories of each other at all.

I was in my early 70's when I met Lillian. She was 65. We had a strong physical connection which propelled us into a marriage after only three months (Holy Moly!). It both frightened and delighted all our adult children.

Since her retirement, Lillian had been developing her painting skills and by the time we met she had organized a studio tour, developed a greeting card line and had a painting space with five other artists. I found the intensity with which she pursued her new-found artistry quite intriguing.

To lure her away from her studio, I proposed a number of exotic travel locations which delighted both of us and allowed me to enjoy her without outside distractions. Her IPhone, however, became her method of chronicling our travels. She said this was a way to keep in touch with friends and gave her an outlet which I guess I didn't provide. Every return home was a gift for her and touching down on the tarmac would elicit her biggest grin. It wasn't just the return to our beautiful west coast city with its clean air and clean streets, but the opportunity to return to her painting. I was beginning to feel Lillian belonged to a bigger world outside of her life with me.

My need for her to be constantly at my side raised questions about feelings of possessive control and paranoia. I know she loved me dearly but still became disenchanted when I would drift off-topic and couldn't follow conversational threads. I became defensive when reminded of this and began to deny my cognitive decline. I still read newspapers but couldn't sustain my memory for novels. Lillian began attending meetings for caregivers of those suffering from dementia in order to deal with my progressing symptoms. My need to still be considered vital compelled me to continue pushing for travel opportunities. Despite the fact I was on several prescriptions to ease anxiety, help with memory and increase libido, my doctor gave me the go-ahead for our last trip. Lillian felt he was extremely negligent by not screening for my growing signs of dementia.

Lillian returned from our final trip on her own.

Over the next two years, I watched Lillian deal with my death and all the emotional upheaval around my repatriation, cremation, memorial, insurance companies, lawyers, notaries, estate and inheritance decisions plus the serious turmoil from my three children. I regret their behaviors because they felt neglected and financially overlooked, but as I always told Lillian, "'My kids will take everything, so I'm goin' out with nothing.'"

Before my final departure, I sent a hummingbird to tap against her window as a last goodbye.

8

MONET'S GARDEN

Following his death, Evelyn now finds her days stressfully filled with settling his estate. These executive decisions need to be cleared away so she can return to a mindlessness which allows her thoughts to wander along sidewalk cracks or aimlessly watch paint colors swirling down utility sinks. The demands needed to address the settling of his estate are considerable; family feuds will hopefully soon end with a final payout.

Previous to Harry's death, Wednesday afternoons, 4:00, had always been set aside for her three closest women friends. For thirty-six years The Amigas had been part of each other's lives. Their 4:00 Happy Hour provided a laugh at aging frailties or guilty indulgences and sometimes, before wine and food, they would bring used clothing and household items in order to rake through each other's cast-offs. Her Amigas had sat as a group a few rows back during Harry's memorial service and showed supportive, sympathetic faces when Evelyn turned to acknowledge their presence.

On this particular Wednesday, Evelyn thanks them once again for everything, after which they share stories about their memories of Harry. Previously, these friends had really only known Harry through Evelyn's stories. Of course, they knew of Harry leading up to the wedding but the whirlwind courtship had been short and the moments to really get to know him too brief. Perhaps they had met him during theatre intermissions, seasonal get-togethers, brief conversations at gatherings, occasional dinner parties. They may have shared travel information or nodded hello doing errands or grocery shopping. Nonetheless, their scant memories are comforting.

A fatal heart attack for Harry, while on a vacation island in Greece, had ended it all abruptly in a most surreal fashion. How could this magnificent landscape be the scene of her most painful personal disaster? They had shared numerous travels during their short married life which provided memories of art galleries and museums, cappuccinos at cozy tables in sidewalk cafes, narrow cobblestoned streets, rude French waiters. Harry and Evelyn had married later in both their lives, being husband and wife for all of two years. Harry loved to indulge Evelyn's passion for galleries and art walks. Historic visitations had made her positively giddy. Castles, with imagined lifestyles, opulent thoroughfares, tree lined boulevards, gentile 18th C. manners, romantic assignations . . . all so inspiring.

Over the years, Evelyn and her Amigas had stood in front of scores of works by famous artists. The gathering of art books for her small home library had become an easy Saturday pastime beginning with garage sales and book fairs. When Harry married Evelyn, she had a studio space located near their apartment. This provided her with like-minded artistic friends and a quiet retreat from her shared small living environment with Harry.

Today, as Evelyn sits with her Amigas in Anna's living room, she looks once again at the reproduction of Monet's "Water Lilies" hanging near Anna's fireplace. She has viewed this universally appealing image on coffee mugs, placemats, journal covers, napkins, table linens and t-shirts. She has even seen a framed poster of this particular "Water Lilies" hanging on the reception room walls of her doctor's offices.

She and Harry had visited that area of France and had purchased ceramics to remind them of their love of that experience. They had arrived in Giverny by train from Paris and rented bicycles to reach Monet's garden. It had all seemed idyllic. Today, gazing at Anna's print, over the array of wine glasses and cheese plates, it takes on an inviting and welcoming calm.

"How I would love to just walk away from all this." she thinks to herself amidst the Happy Hour chatter . . . to simply walk away from my life right now."

Evelyn gazes intently at the Water Lilies print while the conversation sounds fade. She sees a small black hole developing in the middle of the print and watches transfixed as it slowly begins to expand. For her, this moment will always be remembered as smelling strongly of peppermints.

It is a late spring day,1875, and she is walking along a path through Monet's garden. The soil is moist, having just been newly watered. The soles of her shoes are becoming mud-clogged. Flowers are profuse, cicadas buzz and there is a heady mix of floral scents. As she rounds a corner of this amazing pink house, she snags her dress on a climbing rose and bloodies her finger trying to unhook it.

This is Giverny, France, eighty kilometers northwest of Paris. She has entered the garden which Claude Monet is beginning to lovingly create. She is strolling through tightly packed rows of lush spring blooms against a backdrop of his soft pink two-story house with its bright green shutters. This array of riotous garden colorburst fills her completely. Large white and pink peonie heads bob in the fresh breeze. Next to them are banks of purple irises alongside masses of orange and yellow sunflowers, shasta daisies and late blooming tulips. "Not the classical French garden . . . more English styled plantings," she muses as she runs her hand in the air over the many heads of bright orange poppies. The sky is shockingly blue.

The flower garden extends to the edge of one section of his property. Evelyn must then cross a road to reach the famous water lily pond. As she sets foot on the road, a woman cycles past, baguette and wine in her basket and smiles hello.

Evelyn continues across the road and then she sees him. There he is. She's startled. Several seconds pass. She can see him clearly, sitting on a small wicker chair, gazing quietly at the scene before him. He's wearing a brimmed brown felt hat and a light gray, three-piece tweed suit despite the warm weather.

As Evelyn looks past him, it takes a moment before she realizes she is looking at an empty field. Ahead of him, there is no famous water lily pond. There is no perfect, bright green bridge above sparkling water. No tall trees surround the floating lilies. She looks back at Monet who continues to stare straight ahead. His beautifully imagined waterlily pond exists, at this moment, only in his future imagination.

"Camille!" he suddenly shouts to his cook, "Camille! Where are my glasses?"

Evelyn turns to see the cook running from the house carrying his spectacles in one hand and with the other, swatting the bugs which fly about her head.

"Where IS my wife? And where are the children?" he asks again impatiently, taking the glasses from the cook's outstretched hand and hooking the arms behind his ears. "Oh, yes . . . the picnic."

I follow the cook back to the house listening to her muttering gentle curses. She wipes her feet before entering and then lets her hands run slowly down her long white apron. Composed, she crosses the wide-plank floor to the alcoved stove. Bright white and canary yellow tiling patterns are everywhere in this kitchen and are just as startling as what Evelyn remembers. A pot of sunflowers is positioned in the middle of the table around which are placed four mismatched wooden chairs. The cook had been stirring a new vegetable soup before Monet rudely interrupted.

". . . like an old man . . . no manners . . . or memory . . . " she scoffs . . . "*Mon Dieu*". Loaves of warm bread cool on a sideboard.

Leaving the cook to her meal preparation, Evelyn climbs the narrow stairwell off the kitchen to the upper floor and Monet's bedroom. Lining both walls of the stairwell are numerous prints of Japanese woodcuts, one after the other scaling the stairwell walls. She climbs, muddy shoes in one hand. These are hand-pulled prints in bold, bright colors. Heavy black lines outline the shapes. They depict scenes of nature, landscapes and families at the seaside, crowded markets, geishas in bath houses and children flying kites. Monet's bedroom walls are also lined with Japanese woodcut art. None of his own impressionist work is visible anywhere in the bedroom. The furniture here is sparse and simple.

Downstairs, she can hear the cook calling out to him in her shrill voice, *"Monsieur! A table!" "Monsieur . . . s'il te plait!"*

From an upstairs window, Evelyn looks out to see he remains seated by his imagined lily pond. Perhaps he has fallen asleep as his head is bent forward. His bearded chin touches his clasped hands which rest on his chest.

Descending the stairs, she notices the cook has set the table for his noon hour meal. Leaving quickly by a side door, she walks to Monet's studio. A circular area is being specifically constructed to support what will eventually be his massive mural-sized waterlily canvases. These canvases will be attached, one to the other, giving the viewer an impression of being totally immersed in his future water lily scene. How will he describe it? He hopes It will be even more overwhelming than standing beside the actual pond when it is eventually constructed.

This studio has become an important setting over the years for his many gatherings of patrons, friends, townsfolk and artistic colleagues. Monet has developed a close following of renegades and artistic visionaries who are passionate about their new painterly *oeuvre.* Mostly men, with the exception of one or two female artists, their models, mistresses and wives, Monet welcomes them all and excels at hosting. They share a vision of investigating new subject matter, rejecting the strict formalities considered suitable by polite society. They want to explore light and how to apply paint and the delights and problems of painting outdoors. They discuss mutual criticisms or praises of the art world in general and their own financial problems in particular. The rigid rules demanded for the yearly entry into the Paris Salon is a favorite topic which keeps them arguing long into the night. Equally as contentious is the gallery for the rejects, Les Refuses.

An idea begins to form slowly in Evelyn's mind as she stands at the open door to Monet's studio:

"**I** could be the one to stretch his canvases . . . **I** could be the one to clean his brushes . . . **I** could be the one to stir the soup . . . "

THREE YEARS LATER

Anna feels she is fortunate to have secured an early place in line to this highly coveted art show. Anna is the last of her Amigas. She is alone today, as she is almost always these days.

"So wish you were all here," she says to herself.

This gallery tour with her friends would have been punctuated with a stop and a sigh and a stop and a sigh in front of each shared memorable painting. Before leaving the show, they would have made a visit to the gift shop and paid exorbitant prices for hand printed silk scarves. Their afternoon together would finish over a glass of pinot on a favorite ocean-front patio followed by their customary group photo.

Anna now takes note of how the light streams into this newly constructed gallery addition. Her city has been successful in becoming the final west coast stop for this remarkable show: THE IMPRESSIONISTS AND THEIR VISION, *A Showcase Of The French Masters And Their European Contemporaries From The 19thC.*

Anna walks slowly through the two floors of paintings marveling at such beautifully rendered images in their heavily carved and gilded frames. Some are familiar, some are not.

As she stands before Gustave Caillebotte's PARIS STREET, RAINY DAY, she is caught by the expression and posture of the female figure clutching the arm of the man to her right. He wears a top hat and holds an umbrella above both their heads. Caillebotte was one of Monet's many champions of *en plein aire.* The male figure is possibly the more important focus of the painting, however there is something about his female companion which keeps Anna's focus. Her posture? The color of her hair? How she lifts her hem off the wet sidewalk? The impressive architecture of urban Paris is featured in the background, amidst the raindrops. Despite the ornamental portrayal of women in most paintings during this era, this female figure gazes away to her right, indifferently. She shows a familiar half profile. The resemblance is altogether too uncanny.

"How utterly amazing. It's like . . . you are Evelyn's museum doppelganger," she says aloud.

The painter is unknown to Anna so she opens her program: "Gustave Caillebotte (1848 - 1894) was one of the lesser known impressionist artists, given to capturing the banal and everyday pedestrian life of French citizens."

Anna gazes at the painting for a very long time and then turns to look for the exit. As she makes her way to the elevator, something makes her turn back to Caillebotte's work.

"Evelyn," she thinks, . . . "how very much like you she is."

9

PORTAL

Every time she slides her bookcase shelves apart in order to lower her murphy bed, she fantasizes revealing a secret doorway . . . which will lead her down a set of stone steps, to a boat . . . moored underneath the castle at the moat's edge . . . or maybe, instead, this secret doorway will lead her *up* a set of stone steps to a rooftop where she will find a ladder. She will climb the rungs of the ladder easily, hand over hand, feeling no pull of gravity. As she ascends through the cloud layer, she can ju-u-u-ust begin to see the rising sun start to peak over the horizon. Suddenly, a glittering line of very bright sunrise light will race across the waves towards her. Only early morning fishermen have seen that spectacular vision. From the top of the ladder she can now make out several boats of all sizes, sailing past. They are traveling over ocean water filled with spy-hopping whales and leaping porpoises. The people on the boats are clapping their hands and running to the railings for photos.

One of the boats sailing past is carrying many people she instantly recognizes. These are happy revelers she hasn't seen for a very long time. It is the kind of raucous regatta she always associates with "boatie" people. She can hear beer cans being opened and ice cubes clinking in glasses. She realizes she is entering a strange environment not unlike a movie set. Everyone around her seems caught up in the happiest of celebrations. Hugs are abundant and kisses on both cheeks, *de rigueur.*

". . . *such a party atmosphere!*" she thinks . . . *"How unlike life back at the bottom of the ladder! It's like being welcomed into an exclusive sorority (or a weird cult) where everyone wants to share the secret handshake".*

"I feel instantly initiated," she laughs out loud. "Everyone is waving hello! And there are **NO** mean girls!!!" . . .

So, where exactly is she?

This is quite unlike anything she had ever experienced. Passers-by confirm what she is thinking. She is told that all the inhabitants are released from previous emotional constraints. They are also free to roam anywhere unencumbered by physical limitations. And, yes, what she is witnessing is correct: everyone is buoyant.

As she wanders about, deliberating her new surroundings, a subtle "ding" sounds. It is an incoming notification from the device in her pocket. It is really nothing more than an indication of time, which apparently . . . is fleeting.

Families with children need their routines. Homework needs finishing. Lunches need to be readied for the following day. It is not entirely unlike life at the bottom of the ladder. The main difference, however, is the general level of absolute tranquility. Freedom from pain and anxiety are universally experienced. Unsure exactly where to go at this point, she is directed, by several small children, to head into the city center where an apartment is waiting for her.

If ever she were to walk into her dream studio space, this is it. She opens the door to perfect north light flooding the main room. She can immediately visualize herself standing at her easel, the sloping glass skylight at her back. In one corner, by the ornate archway to a small plant conservatory, stands an enormous cabinet for her equipment. A seating area with a chaise lounge and chairs is off to her left. Straight ahead, the kitchen area opens onto a spacious balcony where a lengthy table is positioned under a vine covered pergola. The balcony wraps around to the right and opens into the plant conservatory. The city view from the balcony is breathtaking.

As she stands on her patio looking out over the highrises, she receives another notification to attend an introductory meeting at Central Office. A car is being sent to transport her. Please be downstairs in the lobby, the message reads.

Arriving for the meeting, she sees the CEO and heads of departments casually assembled in a spacious conference room with lots of coffee and assorted doughnuts.

"And how have you acclimated?" the Chief Officer inquires.

"Effortlessly," she answered enthusiastically. "I feel very much at home."

"Good," he replies. In order to make your transition as seamless as possible, we have found it best to provide a brief return in order to say a final *au revoir* to loved ones and friends, of course. Perhaps you'd like to travel. Maybe you'd like to assist strangers through hardship. The choice is entirely yours. We recommend a month of sunsets before you make your way back to us. Give it some thought and we'll send the car for you tomorrow to drive you to the train station."

"The train station?"

"Yes, Silly Rabbit," the CEO replies with a chuckle. "You'll arrive like all our other *messengers*. By the way, choose a name and we'll prepare all suitable documents so you can fit into your new life, rent a car, get a credit card, that sort of thing."

When Celestine Goodchild steps down from the train into her first location, she thinks how nothing has changed. Her appearance is quite altered to facilitate this visit, but really, nothing else has changed. Everything is exactly as she had left it. Her memorial service has already started and is being held in a garden. Between tributes, she easily insinuates herself into conversations with family and acquaintances.

"You always were her sweet tooth," Celestine tells her cherished grandson.

"Put up a bird feeder. She would like that," is Celestine's advice to her beloved daughter. "Also, think of a bird bath."

"Now might be a good time to stop saying such *shitty* things," is her next suggestion to a woman she used to know.

Celestine "hovers" close to her loved ones for several days to oversee their moods and behaviors. She appears as a mail carrier, a window cleaner, a substitute teacher and finally as a grocery clerk. It is so comforting to return for this short while; she can readily see the benefit to all *messengers*. She leaves little goodbye notes in the form of a feather or a seashell on the front steps of their homes. She is the harbour seal whose head pops out of the water while one friend stands at the ocean's edge. She is the bright orange gerbera which is delivered as a condolence gift to her daughter.

When it is time to move on, Celestine feels her next task will be to prevent travel mishaps. Several long-haul truckers are poked awake with a sharp jab to the ribs. One overworked airline pilot falls into a diabetic coma despite her persistence. Fortunately, control of the cockpit is handled effectively by the co-pilot and a safe landing is performed. A locomotive pulling flammable bitumen is diverted from derailment by last minute track adjustments. Several passengers are alerted to a knife-wielding traveler who is subdued and disarmed before the police arrive.

She has done well, she feels, and on her return is immediately ushered into the office of the CEO for debriefing. Celestine knows she could successfully continue this mission if she were allowed to remain at the bottom of the ladder. So, when she makes that request, she is informed of the *Classica Angelicus*. They are a special order of *overseers* granted earthly authority because of their seniority. It seems there is already a hierarchy in place; her place is here for now.

So, life at the top of the ladder resumes. She has bade her final farewells and happily again takes up residence in her sweet home. Many dinner parties are held with friends and family from long ago. Sailing around the harbor happens every Sunday afternoon. How fulfilling it is to reconnect with the sweet men and women who have arrived before her.

She finds she still has a lot of questions about earthly preoccupations like rivalry and jealousy and conspicuous consumerism. It's such a relief to discover they will no longer exist for her.

10

OUR GOOD FRIEND LEO

PROLOGUE:

Leo has been murdered and brutally sodomized during a prison riot. His naked body is discovered in a shower stall, face down, lying atop his pooled blood. The sharpened shaft of a plastic toothbrush is still firmly lodged between his shoulder blades and a broom handle shoved up his anus.

Today, Mary and Leo's mother stand over Leo's grave. Mary feels incapable of shedding a tear. What she does feel is grievous injury for the six years she tolerated Leo's callous indifference. Mother, on the other hand, is filled with memories of a precious young child who would look to her for confirmation of his remarkable beauty and well managed temper.

SEVEN YEARS AGO

"Leo, you're bothering me . . . us. Stop. Please stop . . . Leo."

Mary's words are at odds with her attempts to control her intermittent smile. She is one of four women seated around a bridge table trying to concentrate on the bidding. Behind them, with a video camera held as stable as possible and performing wildly exaggerated side steps, is Leo, her husband.

As he ever-so-slowly circles behind the chairs on which the four women sit, he facetiously comments, "J-u-u-u-ust a moment longer, Ladies. I want to capture all the heightened drama and mounting tension of this incredible bidding process."

L-E-O." This time Mary's tone is unmistakable.

"Does no one appreciate my artistry! Honestly!" he demands huffily, quietly amused with himself. He snaps the camera cover shut and exits the living room.

After retreating to his study, several quiet seconds pass between the four women.

"Leo's new toy?"

"Yes." responds Mary. "For his birthday. From his mother. He often acts the silly buffoon. I guess tonight it's getting on my nerves. Can we review the bidding?"

As Leo closes his office door, he can hear these slightly disparaging remarks from Mary. It's more often what he hears now when he knows she doesn't completely have his back. It's really a minor slight, but for an insecure man like Leo, it resonates as something hurtful. Something he might want to remember.

To look at Leo, one would hardly ever view him as insecure. It was an observation commonly made of Leo that his habit of stroking his well muscled chest was to make **others f**eel insecure. He never passed a mirror without nodding smug approval at his reflection.

Leo has been blessed with a magnificent physique and a shockingly thick head of streaky blonde hair which tumbles attractively over his forehead. He has a stunning smile with a perfect set of white teeth. The strange politics of beauty seem to work in Leo's favour on every level, barring the one glaring anomaly: Leo is an asshole.

Leaving Mary to her bridge game, Leo is now secluded in his office. He has locked the door after he enters. He opens the screen on his video camera and presses the rewind button. Under his breath, he begins his slow commentary:

"A-h-h, and here's Mary's childhood friend and hospital colleague, the lovely Claire . . . Claire, you always look at me . . . like you're smelling something . . . just a bit off . . . did I re-a-a-lly read those signals incorrectly at last year's Christmas party, Claire? . . . and what big romantic catastrophe do you need help with tonight . . . your common-law feckless layabout? . . . he's always good for an hour . . . bending Mary's ear . . .

"And next, we have a long-time, childhood friend . . . Emily. True to form, Emily, your main concern tonight will be about your daughter . . . surprise, surprise . . . and what will you endlessly bang on about? . . . daughter's loss of weight . . . daughter's rowing coach . . . daughter, daughter . . . daughter . . .

"Followed by . . . , Helen . . . newbie to Mary's little bridge group . . . odd plump little duck . . . I keep getting "eyes" from you, Helen . . . why is that? . . . "on" for a quick shag, are we? . . . how remarkably handy that you're my dentist's receptionist . . . "And finally, Mary . . . how loyal your friends are, Mare . . . still mad at me for leaving Mother in your care for another weekend? . . . I'll make it up to you . . . flowers . . . yes . . . always . . . grease those wheels.

It is not a hugely onerous task Leo has asked of her. But Mary really does feel like it kind of is. Leo's mother has always demanded that he be at her immediate beck and call. Not stated as such, but understood. Mary is expected to fill the void when he is away. She rarely complains but feels in this case, after last weekend's trip with the new cycling group and now **this** weekend with the same group of men, that, yes, she should voice her objections. However, she resists and feels she will once more rise to the occasion. Anyway, it is only for a few days.

Four years previously, Mary and Leo had met as students under odd circumstances. One day, walking across their university campus, Mary heard a heated argument behind her. The man in question was being scolded by his girlfriend for repeatedly ogling other women. At first, Mary resists the temptation to turn around and compound his humiliation, quietly congratulating the woman for calling him out on his inappropriate womanizing. But, finally, she does.

"Ah . . ." Mary thinks to herself. "Him. I'm not surprised."

Later, Leo approaches her as she leaves a lecture hall. He tells Mary that he recognizes her because of her distinctive outfit and that she had been the reason for the argument which he knows she overheard.

"Well, I guess I'm now both flattered **and** offended for the sake of your girlfriend's choice of men."

"Yes, it was an embarrassing argument to have anyone else overhear," he answered smoothly, seemingly unaware of his larger social gaffe. "I must watch what I say."

"And what was it you said to make your girlfriend so angry?"

". . . bum like a tame bee . . ."

"And **you** think **you** actually need to be more careful with what **you** say. Stunning bit of introspection, that."

Over the next three weeks, it is obvious Leo is besotted with Mary. She is wary of becoming the flavor of the week. He seems to appear, continuously, somewhere throughout her daily campus comings and goings. Her friends are starting to notice and the teasing has begun. She feels Leo's constant attention is a bit excessive. Perhaps he only pursues until intimacy Maybe this is how he courts: persistently and exclusively. Wear the prey down.

One afternoon as he stands waiting by her bicycle rack, she inquires why she has not met any of his friends.

"Well, we'll have to remedy that, won't we?" he answers, teasing her confidently. "I guess I want to have you all to myself. 'Sides, when my friends see you, I'll have too much competition."

Leo really would have liked to have had more male friends but if he looked closely at his talent for friendship, he would be forced to examine another one of his many personal failings. He had enjoyed a short time with a fellow fraternity brother until he made a poorly calculated move on his new friend's girlfriend. That little betrayal had cost him an invitation to a campus squash tournament and word had soon spread. He knew he would have won that damned contest easily anyway. At no point does it enter Leo's mind that his actions are wildly inappropriate and his lechery is becoming increasingly intolerable. So he gets even by breaking into his friend's locker and planting several small bags of cocaine. Campus security is quick to respond to rumors of anyone dealing drugs.

While Mary realizes meeting his friends may be slow to happen, Leo deflects her request by suggesting that she meet his mother. Leo lives off campus with his mother in an elegant but slightly run down old stone mansion. The evening turns into something not unlike a royal presentation which expects a smart curtsey. His mother has remained seated. Had she actually extended her hand as if it were to be kissed?

"So, Mary, you call my son, Leo. Not Leonard."

"Yes. It just seems to have evolved. And he likes it. So, we feel it suits him."

"Well then, my son will have two names to which he will answer."

Mary hears this rebuke and feels immediately she does not meet expectations. Perhaps she is not tall enough. Or, perhaps, not well enough coiffed. As soon as Leo's mother asks her, "What do your people do, Mary?", she feels on the defensive. After hearing that Mary is descended from Ukrainian pioneers who homesteaded near Ituna,

Saskatchewan, Leo's mother's nostrils look decidedly pinched.

Twenty years previously, Leonard and his mother had emigrated from Australia when he was just starting primary school. Leonard's mother had been raised to be a grand lady with privilege and surroundings befitting the wife of someone in Australia's senior government. Certainly not the simple sheep farmer who had caught her eye one summer evening outside Canberra. Following his sudden unfortunate death during a well dig, Leo's mother decides that she and Leonard will emigrate to Canada. Upon arrival, she immediately seeks out the connections to the moneyed class of 1980's Toronto and by the time Leonard is ten, Mother has remarried, this time into construction wealth. She is accepted hesitantly by her new Canadian family; they are wary of this Australian interloper. On the very day that Leonard turns eleven, she is unexpectedly widowed (an open elevator shaft accident on a new building site), Mother is left exclusively holding the purse strings to an extensive Canadian hotel chain. Eyebrows are raised. Her in-laws are shocked. The ugliness leading up to that elevator shaft death is an unfortunate precursor to Leonard's birthday celebrations. This will be only one of two damaging incidents which will happen to Leonard in his early years.

The first formative experience took place six years earlier when he was five. Upon arrival in Canada, Mother enrolled Leonard in kindergarten where he had a very rude awakening: It was made clear to him that he was not a girl. It was a stark realization for such a little boy. His patient teacher kept reminding him that he "was standing in the wrong line". Repeatedly, he identified with the girls' line in going to the bathrooms or the girls' line for dismissal or the girls' line for book return to the library. Leonard's mother was so totally mortified when informed of this behaviour that she forbade him from ever, EVER revealing this fact. "If you will keep this ever-so-quiet, I will buy you a puppy."

Shortly after Mother's remarriage, Leonard began Grade Four. He had always assumed Mother's deep shame as his own and felt the two of them were firmly complicit in maintaining this secret. In the sharing of something so "unsavoury", Leonard knew his mother as his most trusted accomplice. Sometimes he felt eyes on him, silently questioning some aspect of the way he talked or the way he walked or the way he crossed his legs. He learned to speak in a lower voice especially when answering the phone. He copied the mannerisms of sportscasters or "the jocks" and peppered his speech with what he felt were male-centric affectations.

Mother's indulgences had frequently included shopping trips to vintage-era boutiques. She condoned his purchase of a classic old three-piece tuxedo which allowed him to play dress-up, alternating between Marlene Dietrich and Fred Astaire. When Leonard went through his "Marilyn" stage, he lovingly collected every bit of her available memorabilia. In order to cover up this passion (the abundant number of pink organza and satin dresses alone was astounding) the whole charade is passed off as Mother's obsession. It all came to a crashing halt one night when Mother's new husband arrived home unexpectedly from a hotel construction conference. He found Leonard and his mother sitting side by side, in front of the tv, in bright blonde wigs, full makeup and wearing bubblegum pink chiffon while watching the academy awards.

Mary stands at the front door step, waving goodbye to her three bridge guests. The evening has gone well as usual and their easy conversation has been a welcome change from her working hospital environment. She can see Helen waiting behind the wheel of her car until the driveway clears before backing up. Mary waves goodbye again to their departure as Helen turns off her ignition and opens her driver's door.

Stepping out, Helen says, "Got a minute, Mary? I've something I'm dying to share."

It is past 10:00 p.m. and tomorrow is a working day but Mary beckons her to come back into the house.

"Shall I put on more coffee? Tea?

"Water, please, Mary."

Leo had heard the cars starting up so he emerges from his office. He has spent the interim watching gay porn on an old VHS tape he keeps in a secret drawer. Three hours have simply flown by.

"Uh-oh," he says, "The conflab continues. I'm off to bed."

He takes the stairs off the kitchen two at a time, mumbling to himself, . . . "and I do mean flab."

Mary hopes it will not be another long lament from Helen about weight gain struggles from her thyroid meds.

"The good news, Helen," Mary prompts. "You said you have something good to share."

"It's this." And from her pocket, Helen pulls out a small jewelry box containing a turquoise and diamond ring.

"It's from Evan. A commitment ring he says. I know it's only been four months but I guess Valentine's Day prompted him. Despite all our breakups, I feel he's now more committed."

Mary's gaping mouth seems to say it all. "Yes, it **has** been only a short time. But weren't the two of you warned to not become romantically involved with anyone from your therapy group? Or . . . anyone, for that matter? For at least . . ."

"So, you're **not** in favour of this. Is that what I'm hearing?" asks Helen stiffly, snapping the lid shut.

"Helen, I don't need to tell you . . . he's frail and frankly . . . unstable. You and Evan were in a therapy group because of self-harm issues. But wait, you've had that ring in your pocket this whole night. What does that tell you?"

"That his wife's funeral was two years ago and he's ready to move on. I know the three of you were her good friends, but I'm the one in his life now . . . me!" shouts Helen as she struggles with her coat buttons.

"Think carefully about accepting this ring, Helen. There's a reason you didn't share this with the group tonight. Wait . . . Valentine's Day was two weeks ago. Has that ring been in your pocket since" . . . but Helen has gone down the front steps to her car.

Upstairs, Leo has heard Helen's words indistinctly but pretends no immediate curiosity for the details as Mary enters the bedroom.

"Mary, Mary, Mary . . . why do these wounded sparrows flock to you?"

Mary is reluctant to share Helen's news, knowing how Leo can be indiscreet about her friends. Instead, she decides to confront him.

"Why the song-and-dance with the camera, Leo? Could you not see how disruptive that was?"

"Oh, come on," he replies. "**That** was funny. **I** was **very** funny. **That** was nothing."

"No, Leo. That was not nothing. That was something. I find it happens a lot now. It's the same thing you do to make me lose count when I'm doing my exercises. You have a not-so-subtle way of undermining the efforts of others."

"So glad I'm married to a psychologist," he responds icily and enters their bathroom.

Leo frequently reflects on his early years at university before he met Mary. He might have had a brilliant future as a lawyer but discovered sadly that cheating on his LSATs turned out to be an unnecessary and foolish blunder. He had, however, been able to keep it from his mother by tearing up the gambling marker owed by the invigilating professor who was seriously out of his financial depth. Poker and horses, Leo thinks. Leo has forged his mother's signature in order to make the money transaction, thus providing his professor with the several thousands he requires. At the same time, Leo frees himself from the ghastly social embarrassment which would have reflected poorly on his indulgent mother. That little act of deceit was eventually discovered and cost him the opportunity to enter the faculty of law. Leo sees this as only a slight deterrent. His explanation to his mother is easy:

"Mother," he states calmly, "I do not feel the law is a wholly honorable profession."

Not surprisingly over the years, it seems each selfish decision on Leo's part reinforces his narcissism. He feels entitled to get whatever it is he requires by any means available. He even tried shoplifting a few years ago and discovered he was quite good at it. He lifted everything from a full length Harris tweed overcoat to an expensive cut of chateaubriand.

Leo has always been acutely aware of his ability to manipulate and gives no thought to his complete lack of remorse. People are so gullible. Mother had forgiven him his signature forgery when it was discovered. He explained it as money needed to fix a certain problem with a young woman whom he has no intention of marrying, despite her condition.

"Oh Leonard," Mother had chastised, ". . . do be more careful."

Following that incident, Leo had met Mary. She had won a scholarship to the prestigious eastern university he attended in order to complete her Phd. in Clinical Psychology and Speech Pathology. Leo is now in his final year of an undergrad degree in the Faculty of Commerce and envisions his future tied up in the life of a CEO attending high level corporate meetings and enjoying a corner office. To fully ensure that fantasy, Leo decides to offer his brilliant but financially needy foreign-exchange tutor (how crushing are those student loans!) a very large sum of money to sit his final exams. After the exam marks are posted, Leo is informed about the unbelievably harsh news that his loyal Bangladeshi tutor is hospitalized with serious head injuries sustained in a motorcycle hit-and-run. Those injuries will later prove fatal.

Leo expresses sincere condolences to Amir's family at the funeral while thinking smugly to himself, "No chance now of any future blackmail threat."

Leo's mother is only too proud to supply the ornate frame for his degree which now hangs on the wall in his sixth floor office in one of the many commercial buildings she owns.

Leo is calculated in his decision to ask Mary to be his wife. They have only known each other for roughly six months when this idea begins to take shape. Years of his lecherous campus behavior is known to everyone including Mary. She is described by all who know her as a quality woman. What could someone like Mary be thinking, her friends wonder. He's such a womanizer. He seems to have no shame. He's an unscrupulous philanderer, a seducer.

For Leo, to dispel the gossip, he feels marrying someone like Mary would make his stock soar. He sees it as his opportunity to leave behind numerous romantic dalliances which are beginning to prove awkward. He tells himself he really doesn't like to be such a cheat but every woman he meets makes it so easy. They audibly sigh when he enters a room. The pupils of their eyes visibly dilate, for heaven's sake. He will have to be careful with his flirtations. He knows he has a good thing with Mary.

One of Mary's main attractions is her lack of giggling. He finds giggly women abhorrent. Unfortunately, all too often, Leo's very presence seems to turn most women into silly, eyelash-batting simpletons. Sexual harassment, at this point in history, has not yet become a topical, news-worthy item It's only 2015 and both genders are still evolving.

Leo and his mother fly nine members of Mary's prairie family to their city and host a small but lavish wedding followed by an elegant dinner at one of Mother's fashionable hotels. Mary's family members are housed for the week in two penthouse suites. They are wined and dined and at the end of the week are taken by limousine to the airport. Before departing, Mary's grandmother hugs her and says, ". . . our sweet Masha. We wonder if he deserves you."

Now, three years later, Mary occasionally wonders the same thing.

The next morning Mary is behind the wheel of her car, turning into the hospital parking lot. She decides to get a coffee before heading to her office. As the elevator doors open onto the cafeteria floor, she spots Claire and Emily at a table having breakfast.

"Let me catch you up on Helen's latest news," she says, joining them. "I have to make this quick because I have a meeting. But Evan has given Helen a commitment ring. A Valentine's gift. Helen had it in her purse during our bridge session last night. Didn't tell us. After the two of you drove away, she came back into the house and showed it to me."

The two women are silent. They have had many conversations about Helen since she and Evan met. Their history with Evan goes back two decades when he was married to their much beloved mutual friend. When Evan became a widower, these three women helped to support him through the first two years of his rocky emotional recovery.

After Mary leaves her friends she walks to her office. The first thing she notices as she enters is the slight changes in position of the two small framed photos on her desk. Cleaners. In both photos, taken in their first year of marriage, they show her sparkling, bright smile and eyes. I don't feel like her these days, Mary thinks. Leo is probably right: I have changed. I **am** more critical of his behaviour. I **am** more tense in social situations. I **am** more worried he might say something to embarrass us.

In their newly married days, Leo had been strangely silent when she corrected his grammar and pronunciation. Hearing his mother's same conversational mistakes makes her realize Leo's youth has been spent listening to her frequent mispronunciations. With no one to correct his mother, it was only natural that Leo would pick up on her incorrect speech patterns. She recalls several conversations about these shortcomings and cringes.

"Mary, are you telling me **I** reflect poorly on **you**? All's I said was . . ."

"Leo, it's "**all** I said" . . . not "**all's** I said". These mistakes are telling patterns. And they need to be corrected. You're going into the business of gaining investors' confidence and there are certain expectations."

After a prolonged silence, he replied, "And what else, Mary. Maybe you could make a written list. Small town prairie girl, a child of Ukrainian immigrants, becomes the last word on diction and grammar?"

Mary hated this need to correct him but felt learning to accept constructive criticism was a sign of maturity. She knows she is undermining his confidence and hears the tone in his mother's comment at dinner one night.

"Mary, Leo tells me how you are helping him correct many of his mis-pro-**noun**-ciations. Wait . . . it's pro-**nun**-ciations, isn't it? . . . and, it's "su-thern", correct? not "sow-thern" . . . and "chimney", correct? not "chim-inie" . . . and "re-co**g**-nize", correct? . . . not "re-conize" . . . and "in**t**eresting"? correct? . . . , not "in-eresting." and . . .

At this rebuke, Mary sits in stunned silence. "I see I have overstepped."

Mary is growing tired of Leo's insecurities. However, as the compassionate problem-solver that she was, she feels it well within her capabilities to stroke his ego and still call him out. Leo has always responded well to her tough love but lately, she feels she may be becoming too pushy. She often thinks of Leo's shortcomings as behaviors promoted by his mother in order to feed her own neurotic needs.

To help provide Leo with the sense of leadership he is aching to demonstrate, Mary suggests their combined family finances be placed entirely in Leo's hands. In fact, Leo's mother has also turned her estate dealings over to him. All the holdings from her extensive hotel chain she now gladly places in the hands of her adored son whom she feels has such solid money sense.

Leo really has no aptitude for scholarly pursuits as witnessed by his early actions at university. But he has decided quite early in life, it is far easier to display a well manicured hand free of calluses than to actually toil by physical labor. Hence, his attraction to the business world of white collars and smart suits. He also has an attraction to a largely unnamed need which propels him to amass substantial amounts of money. Perhaps, stock manipulations? Having an acquisitive personality, he sees his self worth grow in simply having "more". Since Leo has set up his new office, he is gaining access to considerable amounts of cash. As an investment broker with a growing reputation, he is able to persuade his mother as well as her many wealthy connections (how he loves to charm those elderly birds!) plus other investors to envision their futures with his careful guidance. He seems to have evaded the recent federal investigation into his insiders' trading move which has benefited his clients to the tune of on average four hundred thousand dollars each. After all, not every insider trade is deemed illegal.

Their initial investments had been small but Leo has a knack for investment foresight. He had inside information on companies developing Artificial Intelligence which he sees as a new opening into the future. Every home will have appliances plus heating and security systems. It is a goldmine potential because all of these home functions will need remote control. A homeowner will need to be able to "talk" to their house. Leo had discovered several companies seeking investment capital. As these companies go public, his clients benefit in ways beyond their wildest dreams.

Two days after the bridge game, Helen sits at the receptionist's desk in her dental office. She is considering Mary's reactions to the news of the ring from Evan. It is still in its little velvet-lined box inside her handbag. Perhaps there is some merit in considering Mary's reactions. Maybe she should further question a relationship with Evan who still exhibits emotional difficulties.

Growing up, Helen never felt she was able to catch the attention of someone like Leo so when he goes out of his way to linger at her receptionist's desk while making a dental hygiene appointment, Helen feels enormously flattered. He seems to hold her gaze for an uncomfortably long time. She has started wearing a new slim-line spanx and feels it is proving well worth the investment.

Helen has enjoyed meeting a new circle of friends. Coming into the bridge group through Evan is both intimidating and exciting. And, as the receptionist for Leo and Mary's dentist, Helen has a small window into another aspect of their daily routines. Leo's office is on the same floor and their cars are also parked on the same parkade level.

"He's ju-u-ust down the hall", she secretly muses to herself, still smarting over Mary's reaction to her new ring. It makes her quietly smile to think she probably sees more of Leo than Mary.

Coincidentally, on that particular Friday, both Helen and Leo leave work early and encounter each other descending in the same elevator. Leo is off to meet his new cycling group for the weekend and Helen is cutting out of work early. They are headed to Parking Level 2 and one thing leads to another. Before Helen knows what is happening, she is in the back seat of Leo's BMW.

After returning to her car, still flustered and disheveled, Helen very carefully drives home. Questions swirl. Every stop light is an agony. She knows she is completely complicit in what has just happened. She reviews their conversations as they emerged from the elevator . . . the sharp edges of the brick wall into which she was pressed when he rushed in for a deep kiss. Now, behind the wheel of her car, she feels only anxiety and panic. After their brief encounter, he hadn't even walked her back to her car. She disappointingly recalls what seemed like a surprisingly short series of quick thrusts followed by the indelible image of Leo backing awkwardly out of his car's back seat, furtively rearranging his suit jacket and closing his fly. In that moment, Helen has the distasteful visual of Leo standing at a urinal doing that exact same clothing adjustment.

"Gotta go, Helen," Leo says. And then, he actually reaches into the back seat and pats her on her knee, saying, "Ah . . . you okay, Helen?"

But her lasting humiliation is walking to her car in bare feet while carrying her shoes. She crosses the cold dirty concrete, her panty hose stuffed into her purse. She unlocks her car and places her handbag along with her shoes on the passenger seat.

There is a red light blinking on her message machine as she enters her apartment. It's from Evan asking her to please call him after work. Helen makes her way to the bathroom and after showering, returns Evan's call, trying to maintain a steady voice. Evan seems oblivious to how she sounds and asks to come over. What he has to say is something he needs to say in person.

"What possibly would you need to tell me in person that couldn't be said over the phone?" asks Helen, feeling the tightness rise in her chest. "Evan, I need an early night." "I'm sorry." I don't feel well and . . . I need an early night."

After several seconds, Evan says, "Helen, I want to be up front . . . I . . . you can keep the ring . . . I don't feel I want to be with you . . . Maybe it's your . . . but I'm really not able to be there for you . . . hell, I'm not even able to be there for myself. It's . . .

But Helen has hung up.

It is pleasing for Mary to come home after work and see Leo's mixed bouquet in a vase on the kitchen counter. This time he has actually remembered to fill the vase with water.

"Stop that, Mary," she says aloud.

Leo must have left his office early. She heads upstairs and sees the evidence of his rapid departure. His suit is hung up poorly and his shirt is in a ball at the foot of the bed. She picks it up and shakes it out, walking toward the laundry hamper. A strong wave of sweet perfume fills the bedroom. She stops, absorbing a new thought. I know that scent, she thinks.

Later, sitting in the kitchen having a cup of tea, she looks at the flowers. She has also discovered distinct make-up and mascara smudges running down the front of Leo's shirt. Plus, a button is missing. The phone rings and it's Leo. He seems particularly happy with his new cycling group. He is phoning from a hostel about 10 miles away along the lakefront. This second trip with the Road Warriors is his entry into the kind of men's group which will help him on many levels. Leo had made a great fuss about acquiring just the right bike plus just the right cycling gear in just the right colors.

"Make sure to phone my mother for lunch at that little teashop she likes," offers Leo. Mary listens to this reminder resentfully before hanging up. She makes no inquiries as to her suspicions. Also, no inquiry has been made by Leo into Mary's general well being at the end of her work week. She knows it's probably the farthest thing from his mind.

The following day she meets Leo's mother at their usual cozy corner table in the little teahouse which has become a favorite meeting place. Mary is always surprised how her mother-in-law makes such a big deal about having to eat alone.

"It's always nicer to share a meal, don't you think, Mary?"

"I guess that depends on who your dinner guest is, Mother," she responds warily.

Leo's mother has repeatedly requested Mary call her "maman" but Mary finds it pretentious. It's only a few minutes into their lunch when Leo's mother makes her usual inquiry. Mary has always quietly agonized over her inability to conceive. Leo's mother anxiously awaits for news every month and never fails to ask questions.

"And where are you in your cycle, Mary? I keep waiting for news of a forthcoming grandchild but nothing yet after these years, it seems."

"You do realize how invasive a question that is, don't you?"

"Well, nothing is going to happen if Leonard keeps leaving over the weekends. Maybe it's time you visited a doctor to see what your problem is."

On Sunday night when Leo arrives home, Mary hears him in the garage putting away his cycling gear. She enters as he's placing his bike up on its wall rack. He keeps his back to her and says, "Please, no questions, Mary. I'm exhausted and need a shower. Talk later?"

Mary has prepared one of his favorite light meals but, for now, she sits at the table alone, a corkscrew in her hand. She hears the shower stop upstairs and waits. A few minutes later, Leo enters the kitchen, toweling his hair. He leaves the towel tented on his head as he makes his way to the sink for a glass of water. He then sits down and slowly lets the towel fall to his lap. Mary looks up from the wine bottle she is opening and lets out a sharp intake of breath. Across the pasta and salad, she looks into Leo's two severely swollen and blackened eyes plus several forehead and nose lacerations.

The following Monday, at about the same time as Leo is being checked out by his doctor, Helen makes the decision to relocate to the west coast. Cutting all ties with her bridge group is easy. The FaceBook de-friending of Mary, Claire and Emily happens quickly. She tells no one except her dental office that she has decided to move closer to her ailing mother. She keeps her vengeful thoughts about Leo's seduction and Evan's rejection deeply hidden. The fact that these two events have both happened on the same evening is a watershed moment for Helen. She feels her humiliation will only be made bearable by leaving everyone and everything behind in order to start over.

Leo's explanations to his wife and his doctor are the same: he was knocked off his bike by a low-hanging branch while riding through a densely forested area. That explanation goes unchallenged. He needs assessments and x-rays on his eyes as well as his brain to rule out concussion. His facial lacerations will mend without scarring and his broken nose will heal with only a slight bump. Spinal contusions have resulted from the whiplash. As well as the X-rays of his skull and eyes he needs several physio treatments. Following the doctor's visit, Mary accompanies Leo to a pharmacy for painkillers and a heating pad. She has made a point of driving the two of them in Leo's car because she suspects that's where she'll find his missing shirt button.

Leo's explanation to himself is something quite different.

He is late arriving at the cycling group's point of departure but no one seems particularly upset. It was the final stop for Mary's flowers which has caused further delay. Also, the episode with Helen in the parkade proved an additional obstacle but in retrospect, too hard to pass up.

It feels like the kind of men's group I've always wanted to be part of, Leo thinks. The plan is similar to last weekend's plan: for the next day and a half, after they leave their cars, they will ride a series of lake trails, stopping at roadside pubs and restaurants along the way. The men will hostel, two to a room. Leo has always heard of this region for weekend getaways as well as day-hikers. It is set picturesquely near fishing camps and casinos. He can hardly wait to tell his mother that he has finally made inroads into cottage country, an area they have always coveted.

On their first cycling night, after he phones Mary, Leo and the five other men check into a hostel and meet downstairs for a late supper. Leo surveys the group and remains quiet. He has learned through past experience to keep his many bigoted opinions to himself until he can assess who the dominant players are. He knows the advantages of aligning himself with the leader. He must quietly and modestly ingratiate himself into a trusted position. He is not to trumpet his personal accolades as he usually does. He will heed Mary's advice and avoid talking over other speakers. He will not shamelessly self-promote.

The next day, they are up at dawn, breakfasted and ready to hit the road. The paths are beautifully laid roadways through extraordinary forested hillsides. Leo is reawakened to an aspect of life he has previously sorely missed. Making money is imperative but the overwhelming pleasures of enjoying physical activity and nature on a sunny day is unparalleled. He feels emotionally full as they stop at noon for lunch.

Buoyed up by a surge of goodwill for his fellow cyclists, Leo feels alive to the pleasant camaraderie around him. Why does he not always feel this way? He is deeply grateful to his client Tom who has introduced him to this cycling group. Fleetingly, he thinks . . . It's such a relief that none of these men know me from my past student life. I have no history with them.

As the six of them sit at lunch, the conversation is casual until the group starts to share personal stories about their childhood nicknames. One of the group, a man named Brad, suddenly turns to Leo and says, "You know what **your** campus name was, Leo?"

Leo doesn't recognize Brad and suddenly feels at a huge disadvantage. He pulls himself into a more erect seated position and scans the men around the table intently. They all stare back at Leo with unsmiling faces.

"I . . . didn't know I had a name," Leo answers slowly, feeling the hairs rise on the back of his neck.

"Well actually, I think you had two," Brad responds. "But the one I knew you by was . . . The Debaucher. It was said you'd screw anything with a pulse so I guess that covers both genders. And the other one was . . . The Perv. Perhaps you recall a certain frat party incident with a drunken pledge brother passed out in an upstairs bedroom? That was my cousin, Leo. That incident had several appalled witnesses."

And, how many women reported date-rape to campus police involving you, Leo?" stated Roy.

Leo's mind swirled, trying first to place Brad and now Roy.

Also, remember your final term advisor, Leo?" continued Roy. "That was my friend's oldest sister."

"What's going on," asked Leo, looking at Tom for guidance.

"And your assault on my niece after a Home-Coming dance?" responds Tom. "And all of us . . . here with you, right now, Leo. You can say goodbye to that pretty face."

They lead Leo outside past the bike stands. After the beating, Leo is told to return to their departure point; he will not be traveling further with the group. Leo has been warned if there is any vandalism to their cars when they return, they will find him and he will receive another beating.

The following day, the Road Warriors return to their cars to find damaged headlights and smashed windshields. Side-view mirrors have been ripped off. Each car has been keyed. They know Leo probably felt fully justified in reciprocating this damage but it was readily agreed by all that he would be made to pay.

Leo's convalescence is slow and appears emotionally painful. He takes almost two full weeks away from his office and spends his days sleeping or sitting on the back porch staring out across the garden. Each evening, Mary arrives home from the hospital to find him in the exact same position as when she left. She makes no overt inquiries into his feelings. Depression is evident. But what has caused such a reaction? Leo's mother remembers a similar aftermath to a hazing episode Leo experienced when he attended an exclusive private middle school at age thirteen. After hearing all the sordid details of the hazing, she immediately removed Leo following a savage fight with the school administration who were additionally saddened to realize Leo's departure meant the removal of Mother's generous library funding. She then enrolled him in a Jesuit school which emphasized academics, leadership skills, public speaking and debating. Leo flourished immediately which restored Mother's faith in organized religion as well as her confidence in what was best for her son.

Buoyed by this insight from her mother-in-law, Mary makes the bold suggestion that they consider relocating to the west coast amidst mountains and ocean and start a whole new life. Mary is happy to leave deep winter snow and summer humidity plus black flies and mosquitoes. Leo is pleased with her suggestion until Mary resurrects the name of their original realtor who found the house they currently inhabit. Leo's brief dalliance with her ended poorly and he has no desire to bring her back into their lives.

"Let's go with another realtor," Leo suggests. "As well, my mother will need to come with us if we relocate. I couldn't bear to leave her behind."

Leo also knows he must make his escape before the cycling group realizes he has flown the coop. Since the Road Warrior trip incident, he has kept their cars out of sight. No telling what those men might further do.

The relocation goes smoothly. Their moving company has them packed up in two weeks and guarantees delivery of all furniture to a newly constructed 12th floor condo in their new ocean-front city on the west coast. They have bought 'sight unseen' on a virtual tour which seems to add to the general sense of great adventure. Leo deliberates trying a completely different business direction. Selling houses might be fun. Some training is needed but entirely "within his wheelhouse" as he tells Mary.

But, for now, he will stay with investment management. Mary leaves her psychiatric administrator's position and feels something will turn up after taking a month or so to settle into their new city. In this new location, Leo's mother buys a penthouse suite on the top of a centrally located office building looking out over the city toward the mountains. Mary's friend Emily is thrilled to buy their house so a realtor is not required. As well, Emily's purchase is ideally located near her daughter's highschool. Leo knows, however, that he must find a new lawyer for the conveyancing because of a similar past sexual indiscretion. So, with houses and cars sold, Leo and Mary along with Leo's Mother fly to their new westcoast city by the ocean.

Happily, Leo and Mary discover several condo neighbors who seem welcoming and are connected to the arts and culture of their new city. Leo meets a group of tennis players among this group who encourage him to join their club. All their new friends are childless by choice, or DINKS as they call themselves, which is a surprising concept for Mary to absorb. They all appear to have vast amounts of disposable income and indulge themselves fully with weekends spent in ski chalets or on houseboats or at fundraisers.

One of Mary's new acquaintances is a headhunter. After discovering Mary's extensive academic credentials, she is presented with several desirable job opportunities. Leo, as engaging as ever and knowing his skill in supplying investment incentives, has a ready audience waiting for his leadership. Managing the extensive portfolios of several new clients provides too easy a temptation for him. Never above considering larceny as a useful means for gaining finances, Leo begins to quietly funnel client money into his own personal accounts.

He's also become interested in the avalanche of real estate purchases from numerous offshore Asian communities. Their newly chosen westcoast city is deluged with construction for the purpose of meeting housing needs for a demanding market in a magnificent location. Soon, the soaring price of condos and residential housing is creating a significant bubble which begins to alarm government sources. Leo sees this as a perfect opportunity to enter the real estate game. He searches out money laundering schemes for illicit funds from a few questionable clients who are buying and immediately flipping properties.

On a recent phone call with Claire, Mary confesses skepticism about their new lifestyle.

"Leo is acquiring all kinds of toys to impress our new friends. It started with a tennis membership and then a large boat and then a yacht club membership and then a quarter ownership in a helicopter. His mother seems impressed."

"Mary, I can hear your concern. How **is** your relationship with Leo and his mother?"

"Much as it's always been. They keep me at arm's length until I'm needed to prop up one of their many appearances. Oddly, it seems I lend my handsome husband great respectability during those moments. He likes to affectionately kiss my cheek when we're surrounded by a large group of people. You know . . . arm around my waist, snuggling in close. Otherwise, we have hardly exchanged more than a few polite words each day since we've arrived. I think I've become his enabler."

After hanging up, Mary hears her own words still ringing in her ears.

Once again, she suspects Leo of being unfaithful after overhearing a conversation while in a bathroom cubicle at Leo's tennis club. Three women are discussing the amorous overtures of a new member which sounds suspiciously like Leo. When they lower their voices and then suddenly burst out laughing, Mary dares not imagine what secrets they are sharing. Leaving the bathroom, she returns to her courtside seat where Leo is waiting for her. He greets her warmly and then waves to the people watching their departure, Mary drives them home in complete silence. Several times she looks over at his profile but Leo continues to stare straight ahead.

In the four years of their marriage, Mary feels a general lack of marital reward. She quietly thinks of their inability to conceive as now, perhaps a stroke of luck. Why would she ever feel a child of Leo's would benefit from having him as a proper role model? But divorce, for a woman like Mary, is hardly a concept she can bear to acknowledge. Her grass-roots, Saskatchewan prairie upbringing has not prepared her for the harsher realities of her new upwardly mobile lifestyle. She has allowed herself to be caught up in something false and pretentious.

The final straw occurs a week later as the two of them are reading the newspaper over breakfast.

"Leo, our housekeeper deserves a raise, I think. I'm going to give her $25.00 an hour starting next month. I'm excited to tell her."

"Well, how much do we now pay her?"

"$15.00 an hour."

"She's lucky to even have a job," he answers curtly, crumpling the newspaper into his lap. "I completely object."

"Leo, be fair. The $15.00 she receives is only slightly above minimum wage."

But he has returned to his reading. Mary turns her head to gaze out the window over the magnificent city view from their breakfast nook. She knows of his arbitrary sense of generosity. Strange how he so readily supported her latest fund-raiser for international medical relief and yet will begrudge his cleaner an added bonus.

"Of course," she thinks. "An unsatisfactory lover **and** stingy."

In a nearby west coast office building, during her lunch break, a newly appointed government secretary takes note of a newspaper photograph of a charity event showing a certain philanthropic couple raising money for Doctors Without Borders.

"Well, hello, Mary and Leo," says Helen (. . . we remember Helen).

At this time, the Attorney General's office has been gradually alerted to the misdeeds and illegal activities centering around money laundering connections to the west coast real estate market. In order to investigate the records of realty offices and brokerage firms, transactions from the previous five years are being subpoenaed and scrutinized. Off-shore interests in high-end real estate acquisitions are becoming front page news. Facilitating the flipping of newly purchased real estate for significant profit is going unchecked.

In her new position, Helen now makes sure that Leo's name and that of any associates are earmarked for legal scrutiny. Helen . . . still flummoxed by her choices in men. Helen . . . still feeling the victim. Helen . . . quietly vengeful. She finds a certain comfort gained in being able to notify agencies to investigate Leo's questionable dealings. His phones are wiretapped and several officers put on his case to surveil his financial dealings.

It takes almost a full year to have the final proof needed to arrest Leo. It happens one evening at his yacht club in front of a dining room full of shocked observers. Leo is taken into custody and given an ankle bracelet since he is deemed a flight risk. He is eventually handed a harsh sentence of 10 years which will be reduced if contrition is observed and community service demonstrated. Leo is being charged with 11 counts of gross malfeasance of private accounts and retirement funds. He has embezzled money from trusting friends and clients. Additional charges of his involvement in money laundering are to be forthcoming.

One evening, before Leo's Incarceration, Mary and his mother are finally able to coerce his full confession in a series of tear-filled rants. As they listen to his twisted rationale, he can not meet their eyes and keeps his head lowered, focusing on his ankle bracelet. His incessant whining elicits a sharp realization in both women as to the extent of his betrayals.

It seems especially hard for Mary to acknowledge her husband's guilt for such deceitful white collar crimes. It is discovered that Leo has helped himself generously to his clients' accounts in order to enrich his lifestyle. He has absconded with over three million dollars from the savings of trusting friends, family and business associates. He has carefully placed all his new acquisitions (a yacht, a helicopter, a ski chalet, an apartment building, two cars, their condo) in Mary's name so she is left appearing complicit in his business decisions. It is now Mary who liquidates all their mutual holdings in order to reimburse Leo's investors (even his mother) at 30 cents on the dollar.

Two years later, Mary and Leo's mother meet for a drink. It's Thursday and Mother has just begrudgingly returned alone from her weekly prison visit. Over the two years of Leo's imprisonment, Mary has refused to accompany her on these visits. Leo's mother always lets Mary know her disappointment by well placed glaring looks and indignant sniffles.

"I'm so surprised that Leo has lasted this long . . . in a prison situation . . . amongst men so prone to violent acts," offers Mary slyly.

"Mary, whatever do you mean? There's a high level of policing. I've talked to the warden. Are you saying he's in danger?"

"Just knowing how manipulative Leo is, I'm surprised, that's all. Nothing should shock us, Mother, about how Leo is surviving on the inside. He's good about setting people up for a fall . . . or setting one person against another . . . I doubt Leo will be alive to serve his full sentence," she finally adds, carefully watching Mother's reaction.

"Mary . . . what are you saying? In all the times we've been together . . . you can't possibly be . . . we're talking about my son, Mary, for heaven's sake!"

"You think because I'm too nice, that I'm too sweet . . . that I couldn't possibly be . . . what . . . involved in . . . ?"

"Well . . . yes," Mother answers. "I'm horrified."

"The same thing could be said about you, Mother," Mary responds coldly.

"What **are** you saying, Mary! **I'm** not capable of **. . .** having someone **murdered!** if that's what I think we're talking about."

"Ah, come now, Mother. Leo told me about witnessing the incident with the elevator shaft when he was a young boy."

The long pause is now punctuated only by Mother's sharp intake of breath, until Mary breaks the silence with, "I've heard it said that we're **all** capable of murder. We just haven't met the right person."

11

THE VIEW FROM MAGGIE'S FRONT PORCH

. . . is across a mixed crab grass and gravel patch driveway where several old derelict cars, car parts, engine blocks, car interiors and consoles lay in scattered disarray. They have sat there night and day, for at least the six months since Maggie has lived here with Ray, They have never been removed or further dismantled, gradually accumulating as if by some secretive morphing of one discarded object into another. Ray has no immediate need for any of them, nor any part of them, but, as he always assures her, "You never know."

His side hustle as a part time grease monkey maintains his weed habit while his actual paying job provides a monthly cheque which includes medical and pension benefits. It's a union job at the mill. He had gone into the mill straight after graduation. His whole family are mill employees.

Ray's hoarding habits are unknown to Maggie when she first "takes up" with him. She is seventeen, newly graduated and as equally smitten with his hard 6-pack as with his hot orange and red Trans-Am. Roy had been four years ahead of her in school. When Maggie meets him again at a beach party, he seems worldly and knowing. He has a vague recollection of Maggie as one of his younger sister's many girlfriends who would hang around while he pumped iron in the backyard. He remembers them peeking around kitchen curtains, their fingers covering shiney braces as they giggled.

At the time of Maggie's own graduation, Ray had become peripheral to her intentions. She had plans for her life.

But here she is now, a year later, after that beach party, living a common-law experience with a man whose six-pack is becoming less cut and whose front yard more cluttered. For Maggie, that beach party was her final grade XII fling and the beginning of her process in making an application for a nursing degree program. She had prospects. She had a plan for her future. And then she had met Ray and feels now that perhaps she's been sidetracked. At least she and Roy have wisely decided to simply shack-up. And now they are approaching that legal tell-tale twelve month mark which will alter their relationship status. A fork-in-the-road moment.

Maggie, now reunited with Ray's family, sees them in a different light. At first, she denies the dysfunctional morass she is entering but slowly begins to realize how Ray is part of a whole package along with his entire family. Father is unsmiling, short-tempered and sullen; Mother is more light-hearted but hesitant and suspicious. They are guarded but still generous in their affection for Maggie. They never miss an opportunity to remind Roy, "Son, you are over-achieving with this one."

Maggie finds these statements uncomfortable on Roy's behalf and marvels at his resignation in accepting their jibes. His family seems largely uncultured and are oddly proud of it. Not a single one values her pursuit of a nursing degree. What they value is money and how to make more. Does nursing provide money, they would inquire? How many years until you get that degree, Maggie? How long will it take to pay back those costs?

Maggie herself does not dislike money. Far from it. But, as the carrot at the end of the stick, it represents empty satisfaction. She wants to be a professional. She also wants the additional educational experience.

The morning she buys the lottery ticket is pretty much like any other grocery day. The winning numbers will be posted that night. She had just made it under the wire. By 6:00, Maggie has checked and rechecked her ticket against the website's posted winning seven numbers. She holds a winner, she realizes. SHE HOLDS A WINNER!!

She thinks she might have to share it with the others who hold the same numbers but dividing $16,000,000.00 is hardly crushing.

She sits on her usual front porch step staring down the length of the many discarded car parts, the lottery ticket in her hand. In the distance she can see Ray's vehicle turning off the main road. She waits for him to gun the "Flaming Red Menace" through that depressed muddy area where their gravel driveway curves. He skirts the assorted engine parts and tire stacks and comes to a stop directly in front of her. Music is blaring at maximum pitch which cuts off abruptly when his engine quits.

Ray slowly opens his car door and sits for a moment before stepping out. When he does, he has a wide smile which is not his customary face after returning from the mill. Ray hates his job. He works the green chain. It is extremely lucrative but fraught with danger and excessive industrial noise. His family connections have provided him this opportunity but after five years, he wants a different lifestyle. Mill life is rough. The people are rough.

Growing up in a factory town over several generations creates a "stick-it-to-the-man" mentality. When the shift horns sound, machinery stops immediately. Not one scintilla of energy is ever expended past that signal. Does that provide pride in one's work? Not really. These assembly line jobs are repetitive and mind numbing but woe unto those whose thoughts are allowed to drift. Accidents happen.

He wasn't disdainful of what his parents had provided. Ray has grown up in a beautiful home on magnificent ocean front property. He has entered salmon derbies since he was a boy standing alongside his younger brother and sister in the stern of his father's 35' Bayliner. He has water-skied and wake boarded during the summers and snow boarded their neighboring mountain in winter. Ray knows his parents have worked hard to provide for their three children. And they never let him forget it.

Ray and his siblings are the first in three generations of their family to graduate from highschool. Despite the fact that Ray has overheard his parents refer to him as "not the sharpest tool in the shed", he feels he has a destiny past employment in the mill. Ray knows he wants to be a civil engineer. His parents listen patiently while he outlines his plans, stopping him only when he mentions the money needed to finance his five years of campus life. Getting the mill position was only to be a means to an end. But as the years have gone by, his goal of civil engineering drifts into the wind like so much cannabis smoke.

And then he meets Maggie. She has plans for her life and he likes that. She says her job at the fish packing plant is just to give her the funds to pursue her nursing degree. Same as Ray. They have ambitious plans to head to higher learning but with each passing season, they feel the goal posts are being moved further downfield. Admittedly, they know it is personal lethargy fed by a combination of negative self-talk and lack of family and friend support.

"Whatcha got there, Ray?" Maggie prompts, after taking in the unexpected grin on his face.

"Our ticket to Escape-Ville."

"Me too!" she squeals, "See this?" she says waving her small paper.

"Maggie? . . . Am I looking at a lottery ticket?"

"I'm not sure how many other ticket holders have this exact number but I think by the time the total is divided, we'll have a vision of what paradise can look like."

Ray crouches down beside her on the top step, both of them staring at the papers in each other's hand. Ray's winner is a scratch ticket and has resulted in three symbols revealed for $250,000.00. Unsure of what Maggie's ticket is worth hardly deters their jubilation. They stare at each other in tearful disbelief and then both stand up to dance and gyrate insanely.

They decide to add the two tickets together and equally split the sum. Whatever that turns out to be is a total which can instantly meet both their tuition needs with *a shitload* of room to spare for every other pipe dream imaginable. It is decided that each will have full authority over their individual portion. Knowing an immensely important decision is being made, they also feel a lawyer is necessary.

The two of them talk long into the nights for the first two weeks following their miraculous windfall. They decide to wait a full month before sharing the news. In the meantime, after finding their lawyer, they cash in their tickets, divide their winnings and make a trip to the bank for deposit.

Remaining absolutely silent begins to prove a sound decision. The newspapers announced these winnings as local but decline printing the winners' names. In such a small town, watchful eyes are alert to anyone making sudden, uncharacteristically large purchases. Both Maggie and Ray continue on the assembly lines at their respective jobs. Each has a niggling fear that once the news gets out, they will be assailed with requests from real estate agents, car dealerships, entrepreneurs seeking investment capital not to mention friends and family. They have also read too many horror stories of lottery winners who have blown through massive winnings and been left penniless after only a few years.

Maggie has only her mother to consider when she and Ray break the news. She gifts her mother with a beautiful piece of cliff-top acreage and plans for construction of a mid-century modern 3-bedroom home, artist's studio and garden. No expense will be spared and employment will go to local industry.

Ray's family sit in stunned silence when told of his winnings. They are pleased for Ray and Maggie, but show obvious displeasure for at least not being included in the secret right from the beginning. Ray's father is the first to make a financial request for help: paying off their mortgage. Ray's mother feels that since Maggie is giving her mother a new house on prime property that Ray can at least provide his own mother with a new car. Ray's younger sister wonders if Ray can give her the cash needed to open a nail salon. Ray's brother says he has his eye on a Kobota backhoe which he would use to start a business digging out septic fields. Father also mentions what a nice gesture it would be if Ray could see his way to purchasing the whole family a new boat as well as a possible downpayment for a ski chalet.

That night as Ray and Maggie sit on their front porch, they talk about Ray's family.

"Did anyone inquire about **your** ideas for the money, Ray?"

"Nope . . . for someone they don't consider "the sharpest tool in the shed", they seem unaware that I may actually **have** plans."

Together, they wonder if this Is what happens within a family when one person wins a lottery? Is there an obligation to share? On a grand scale? And how much? Is it appropriate to ask for a gift?

Ray's mother phones the next morning and mentions Ray's uncle could also use some help with the purchase of his yearly commercial fishing license. Ray's uncle's daughter, cousin Charmaine, is getting married soon and a little money tossed her way would ensure a live band and a chocolate fountain at the reception. Ray's sister has found the perfect mall location for her nail salon but she has to move quickly on signing off for a year's reduced rent or the location will be taken over by a tropical fish and aquarium dealership.

"Wish I'd continued keeping it a secret. It's like being pecked to death by ducks."

After Ray instructs the lawyer to give each of his family $20,000.00, he researches the various university programs for entering engineering studies and settles on a highly reputable school as far away as possible from his family. Maggie resurrects her nursing application and discovers she needs to improve her science grades and remedies that new prerequisite by enrolling in Distance Learning. Both quit their factory jobs and pack up their belongings.

Ray is at odds with what to do with all the assorted engine parts and abandoned cars littering their rented front yard property but finds a friend who is only too delighted to adopt a ready-made scrap yard. Moving is the only option for Maggie. She knows she needs a new view from a new front porch.

Ray and Maggie decide to go their separate ways until each has secured the academic future they desire. They will stay connected and cheer each other on as they work toward their separate goals.

Ray's first few months away from his family prove to be a wonder for his personal growth. He secures a private dorm room on a prestigious campus and begins to live a quiet, studious existence. He makes a few friends and develops a social life. His marks are only satisfactory but he feels pleased with exam results. It has been difficult to kick-start himself into action following his years of sweet indolence. Too much pot has noticeably turned his brain mushy. It had seemed so much easier to just blaze up a doobie and let everything slide.

Surprisingly, he rarely thinks about his windfall money. He knows it is quietly gaining interest and will be waiting for him after graduation. He lives frugally, only withdrawing what is needed. He feels it a secret mission to defy the expected outcome for lottery winners.

Maggie's first year is not dissimilar to Ray's. She lives with three roommates in a spacious old house close to her own campus in a different city. She keeps largely to herself, studies hard and maintains a strict private code of secrecy regarding her finances.

Once a week they reconnect by phone and catch each other up. Maggie offers Ray the emotional counterbalance needed to understand how his family has kept him close and dependent all those years rather than encouraging him to seek a life outside their influence.

In Ray's family's emails, they don't hide their displeasure with his decisions. They know that Maggie has been instrumental in persuading him to seek a more independent and academic life. Ray's mother says to him one evening during a phone call, "Ray Honey, is there a possibility for an additional gift of cash like the amount you gave us before? . . . for each of us? Maybe include Dad's brother again and cousin Charmaine along with her new husband? That only seems fair . . . right? It would be most appreciated and we think well within your means . . . right? Could you possibly see your way clear to giving each of us another . . .?

Ray instructed his lawyer to make that happen and then returned to hitting the books.

In December of that first year, Maggie and Ray fly back home to spend Christmas with their families. Ray rents a 5th-wheel RV for himself and Maggie which he parks on Maggie's mother's new property rather than feeling pressured to accept his own family's offer of their guest room.

Christmas Eve dinner at Ray's house becomes an uncomfortable exchange of brittle jocularity and hushed inquiries into what Ray constantly overhears as his "plans for the money". Christmas Day is spent with Maggie's mother who has always run interference between Maggie and any long lost relative/friend/past acquaintance or entrepreneur/teacher/realtor/coworker who wished to make contact with her.

The most distant relatives and children of distant relatives begin to be added to Ray's list after word from Ray's parents spreads. By the time Ray is finishing his first year at university, he is supplying fourteen family members with a yearly "stipend".

Ray then makes a new dispersal decision and directs his lawyer to supply the whole family with one LAST lump-sum amount which they can divide, in whatever way they deem most equitable. He is growing sick and tired of the demands on his generosity. Cash cow, indeed.

Two years later, this new dispersal decision turns out to be the major wedge driven between Ray's father and Ray's uncle. It seems Ray's parents had hoarded the entire gift for themselves (online gambling) since this decision was made. This "unwarranted selfishness" becomes the turning point for Ray's uncle's immediate family and now no one is talking to Ray's parents.

As their gambling debts begin to pile up, the loss of Ray's parent's primary residence is becoming a frightening possibility. Both his mother and father are now barred from the two casinos near their town. Ray's sister has lost ownership of her nail salon because of sloppy health code violations and Ray's brother's backhoe business has folded due to several liens against his license. Cousin Charmaine's wedding has ended in divorce and she has now appealed for help to support her unborn child.

Present Day:

Both Maggie and Ray have now graduated. Today, Maggie's mother sits on her favorite tropical beach sipping her second Pina Colada. She has removed her beach hat and taken off her sunglasses. She is intently watching the horizon for that special moment when the setting sun seems to drop abruptly into the ocean. Ray and Maggie are due to arrive on the evening flight. They'll spend the following vacation month with her in their little rented casita outside the capital city. Living in Costa Rica for the winter and spending the rest of the year back home on her clifftop paradise is the dream retirement which Maggie and Ray have gifted her.

12

ADAM'S APPLE

Ruth-Anne is on a rant. "Why is it that Eve **always** gets the short end of the stick? How can anyone passively read the creation story without seeing her served up as the eternal scapegoat? Aren't they both equally responsible? Like . . . come on . . . temptress? betrayer? manipulator? Snake aside, she will always serve as womankind's failing."

We're sitting out by the lacrosse box after school. Over the summer holidays, our highschool received enough money for a back field upgrade which has meant new surfacing for a 6-lane track oval as well as construction for three new tennis courts. Very cool for a "have-not" school.

We're located in the rough area of our very pretty oceanside city. Lots of drugs and dealers of drugs. Lots of low-cost rental apartment buildings, several half-way houses for unwed mothers or newly released felons. And in amongst all of this are areas of "sound possibilities for gentrification" as the real estate kings trumpet.

"So," I ask Ruth-Anne, "Why this latest?"

"M-i-s-t-e-r Adams . . . possibly THE most obnoxious of teachers. His use of the sly and sarcastic comment leads to such insulting discussions. He positively salivates when he can stir the pot . . . a truly unworthy teacher."

"And you rise to the bait every time."

"And I rise to the bait every time," Ruth-Anne sighs.

Even I find it off-putting when a teacher loads an inflammatory discussion in order to "make us think", as Mr. Adams always defensively states. Nothing seems to get her goat more than the arrogant attitudes of male superiority coming from his "fat bald face" . . . Mr. Adams with his pale sad calves and his bloviated biases". (her words, not mine.)

"Why, Ruth-Anne? Why does this happen after every history class? It sets you off for hours."

By Grade 12, Ruth-Anne and I have been best friends for six years. We had both arrived as late-entry students in the middle of our Grade 6 school year and instantly recognized another true outsider. It was an odd partnership to anyone but us.

I represented the un-spectacular and un-special. I was the before-picture of the make-over reveal. Sad, but true: acne-prone, ragged-cuticles, unibrowed, oily T-zone. I was always hopeful for a late blooming. Growing up, I had agonies concerning my adolescent face. But, Ruth-Anne? Ruth-Anne represented everything that was physically magnificent: She was that face and body over which every schoolboy drools. She sauntered, nay . . . cat-walked through our locker-lined junior highschool hallways like an angel-winged Victoria's Secret runway goddess. Wielding such sexual power must be the headiest of experiences, I thought. How does someone with that much visual appeal deal with the knowledge of what she possesses?

As of today, our friendship has endured all the way into our senior years. At the time of this writing, Ruth-Anne and I are now both in our early 80's. I live in a separate suite adjoining my daughter's house. Ruth-Anne lives in the same city, in a very high end residential, long term care condo. On our weekly visits, we spend most of our time sharing a bottle of wine and pouring through old yearbooks from our student newspaper.

In our Grade XII year, Ruth-Anne and I headed up our school newspaper called <u>High School Confidential</u>. (Yes, you're right. We confess to ripping off the name from Rough Trade's 1981 hit.) We had a smattering of student reporters and one teacher volunteer. We presented monthly columns on relevant subjects like our school's underground music scene (read Tim Olyfeski's garage band) and panel discussions like . . . our school's policy which states that Family Life should only be taught by married teachers.

Aside from Ruth-Anne's desire to set fire to her most un-favourite history teacher, we tried to offer insightful feminist commentary on lofty subjects far outside our experience. But with the hubris of youth, we felt the urgency of voicing our ill-formed opinions and our student newspaper provided a ready format.

We wrote several commentaries after reading the 1960's Betty Friedan book, <u>The Feminine Mystique.</u> In fact, it inspired us to search out other feminist writers who influenced our thinking on everything from challenging our school's curriculum choices to questioning our school's dress code. Mrs. Anderson (patient, eye-rolling teacher-advisor) felt it was important to perhaps soft-pedal our words when it came to terms like "overthrowing the patriarchy". We complied, but maintained an unrelenting undercurrent of dissatisfaction against anything that remotely resembled dominant male control.

During the last six months of our senior year, it was revealed that Mr. Adams was having an extra-marital affair with one of our classmates. It seems they exchanged intimate letters on a daily basis which was revealed (in full detail . . . holy crap!) via social media. And by the time of our graduation ceremonies in mid-June, Mr. Adams was noticeably absent from all faculty events. It seems he had unintentionally assisted Ruth-Anne in her desire to witness him setting himself fully ablaze. He had self-immolated. For Ruth-Anne, it did provide what she wanted for vindication of her feelings about him. But, on the other hand, she felt intense sympathy for his wife and two grown daughters. Ruth-Anne imagined a scenario in which Mr. Adams and his wife would proudly view their yearly Christmas family photo gallery (each an 8" x 12" color print in a solid mahogany frame) which (she also fantasized) lined the wall leading up the stairs off the entryway into their tidy suburban home. What would that staircase display represent for that family now? And how would his two adolescent daughters feel about marriage and men in light of their father's philandering ways when they themselves were the exact same age as his workplace dalliance?

Our school newspaper was given very strict instructions to avoid any reference to this scandal but our student-body grapevine provided easy access to all details. One of the letters in question had apparently fallen from a side pocket in Mr. Adams' bookbag. It had been found by a disgruntled student who desired revenge for a classroom humiliation at the hands of Mr. Adams. The student had then posted the letter's full contents for all the world to see. For Ruth-Anne and me, it opened many conversations into the complicity of sexual attraction. What was it about this particular girl which led to her entanglement with a man like Mr. Adams? Why would Mr. Adams risk blowing apart his family for an adolescent fling? The girl's parents quickly moved her to another school. Mr. Adams was sued by the school board for enticing a minor and completely discredited by his teachers' union. It was later reported he had taken a job selling booze in one of our government liquor board outlets. They had both been forced out in an act of shunning. Expelled from the garden.

"Why isn't this the kind of discussion we should be having in Family Life?"

"A smart suggestion, yes, but obviously not possible," Mrs. Anderson countered. "No one would condone such character assassinations. A better topic might be the ruinous aspects of Facebook and Twitter which allows widespread opinion to violate privacy."

Ruth-Anne and I were always on a quest to understand more about life and love. Mr. Adams and his damaging lack of responsibility was a lesson learned.

For the two of us, we had remained relatively virginal throughout highschool for what I suspected were very different reasons. I suffered from such a lack of confidence in my appearance that I had given up on any possibility for my hoped-for-late-blooming. For me, menstruation didn't begin until I was almost seventeen. Very late by any standard. I was so ashamed of my lack of womanhood that I had lied about it amongst girlfriends at slumber parties for years.

Ruth-Anne, as it turned out, had experienced the exact opposite. She had been forced into "withdrawal" because of an over-abundance of attention which had occurred throughout her entire life. It seems to have started when Ruth-Anne was a very little girl. Her mother recognized the threat an uncle posed as unnaturally attentive. He liked to have his little niece on his lap far too frequently. Ruth-Anne once told me she recalled witnessing a scene in which her tiny mother, with a shaking index finger, confronted her very tall uncle about these suspicions.

So, both fear and shame had rendered us impotent, so to speak. An odd conundrum. At a time when most adolescents were dealing with raging hormones, our sexual urges were in lock down. How was it we were EVER to learn about men, we would wonder.

We had absolutely no money when our outrageous European travel ideas began to take shape in our senior year. It did, however, provide the needed excuses for avoiding boyfriends. The waitressing options in our tourist town were plentiful. We both continued living in our parents' homes so they considered free room and board as their contribution. My mother was only too happy to watch me take on several jobs in order to gather what we considered our 'start' money. Ruth-Anne and I went from waitressing shifts to retail shifts to office temp shifts to bartending shifts and back to waitressing shifts. The service industry jobs were of course the best paying because of the tips but for Ruth-Anne, sexual harassment was often a factor. She told me she grew increasingly more brave about confronting co-workers or employers with a withering remark for their wandering hands.

We crisscrossed Europe by plane and train and took many precarious ferry trips through the Greek islands on leaky old boats. We had even squeezed in a month touring Morocco. We watched bullfights in Spain and Portugal, rock concerts under Norwegian northern lights and celebrated our 21st birthdays in Istanbul by dancing on tabletops with burly men who hardly spoke English. I had finally lost my virginity on an overnight train into Austria. This had occurred at the same time as Ruth-Anne's violent vomiting (too much raki) could be heard coming from the ladies toilet across the corridor.

And now, I was returning from Holland alone. Ruth-Anne had made a decision to remain in Amsterdam as she had fallen in love with a pastry cook and was persuaded to stay. When we stood in the departure area in Schiphol's airport, promising constant emails and messaging, we had no idea that she would be following me just four weeks later. It seems, shortly after my departure, she discovered her new love in the alleyway behind his bakery with one of his coworkers, his pants around his ankles.

After her return, Ruth-Anne began constantly juggling so many invitations that whenever the two of us shared romantic information, the name of her current paramour had changed. She became quite smitten with one fellow in particular until he presented her with a shiny new red sports car. He prompted her to look inside the glove compartment which contained a small velvet box and a massive diamond ring. She loathed that sort of "love-bombing" and knew it instinctively as a form of abuse. She had often witnessed proposals made in crowded restaurants and felt enormous discomfort. As if unconsciously alerted to her greatest dread, one of her boyfriends asked for her hand in front of a stadium filled with hockey fans. Her mortification was doubled for all to see when she looked up at the Jumbotron and saw her own magnified shocked face.

Our lack of fortitude for relationships and marriage was our one area of continuous mutual puzzlement. Ruth-Anne and I had both come from childhood homes of widowed mothers so we felt a distinct lack of male involvement as we grew up. Perhaps this was one of the missing puzzle pieces? We were always amazed by what we observed in the marriages of others: some long-suffering; in others, outright disdain. Truly happy unions seemed largely elusive.

But in the other areas of our lives, Ruth-Anne and I had each created careers which had provided great satisfaction and good incomes plus all the creature comforts we would ever need. We each had failed at marriage(s) but happily had become mothers and then grandmothers. We tried not to dwell on the physical disappointments and betrayals of our aging bodies, but neither of us experienced chronic pain or cognitive decline, so we thanked our good angels for that.

At 80, our lives are now a long way from our younger twenty-year old selves. Whatever we had learned about men and marriage over our lifetimes could now hardly cover the head of a pin. We often share a chuckle about our own seamless compatability.

"It's too bad," she mused one day, "that we weren't gay. We would have made such a lovely couple."

13

MALCOLM WHO LIVES UPSTAIRS

As an agoraphobe, Malcolm has sentenced himself to isolation and the interior of my house. I rent Malcolm the attic (2 huge rooms) of my old Victorian and find him to be an exemplary tennant. As well, he's a germaphobe, so no prolonged hugging or hand shakes. Never far from a bottle of hand sanitizer. "Also, an e-shewer of shoes," he adds. I watch him as he cackles gleefully at his own playful word humor. Hence, no audible footsteps; rarely do I ever hear him moving about. A floorboard might inadvertently creak and then I'm reminded I have Malcolm above me. Unless, of course, he's wearing his high heels.

When Malcolm first answered my advertisement, he started off by telling me odd random personal facts. Height 5' 9", weight 135 lbs., plus the 394 times he has played Wordle, NY Times. His personal statistics show he is able to solve the mysterious 5-letter word, on average, by the 4th attempt. He's still hoping for the day when he guesses the actual word right off the bat. In the meantime, he's always on high alert for new 5-letter beauties, being currently fond of "avoid", "abyss" and "butte". Always on the lookout, he says, for words with good vowel combos.

It made for an unusual first meeting. He spent more time inquiring about **my** circumstances (financial and marital) than about my inquiries into **his**. The oddity of that first interview seems to have set the tone for our relationship and over the years I have come to feel like I'm the tenant and the house belongs to Malcolm.

When Malcolm moved into my three storey, drafty, facing demolition, decaying stone mansion, he said it looked like the perfect Halloween haunt if ever there was one. I had to agree and a decade later, after the extensive rewiring and replumbing, I have currently taken a break from this endless renovation. Malcolm's consistent rent (over ten years) plus financial help from the local heritage society plus my teaching job has made this renovation possible. As it stands today, the interior is "getting there". The exterior wooden portions are still peeling paint, the stone work needs moss removal, the chimneys need repointing, two windows remain boarded up, an "off limits" sign is hung across the kitchen veranda due to excessive wood rot, and several "careful where you walk" garden pathways need work. But, the front and back staircases have been rebuilt (insurance code and fire escape necessities). For the many years in which I lived entirely in the main kitchen and butler's pantry, I feel it's come a long way.

Two servants quarters had originally comprised the attic floor, with each sharing a quaintly positioned water closet. Somewhere along in its renovation history, a garishly coloured turquoise toilet and sink had been installed, a telltale aesthetic from the 70's. This was the very first reno job I tackled because I needed to update the plumbing. I knew I'd never be able to lure a tenant unless I could provide a sumptuous bathroom so I went at it like crazy.

When I found this once beautiful old house, I could see past the raccoons in the attic and the 20-odd cats owned by the eccentric old widow who was the current owner. All her cats were greatly loved and each had a particular window perch which seemed to be a necessary condition for the sustained tranquility of this feline household. This was according to the realtor who said the old woman was about to be forcibly moved into residential care by her three concerned children. I promised her that I would lovingly look after **all** her cats as if they were my own which greatly soothed her. With that stipulation in place, the old mansion became mine. Luckily, I had accidentally hit on a high-return sportswear company investment by complete happenstance and was able to meet the stringent down payment demands. Malcolm just felt like the right fit after that oddly circumstanced purchase. Besides, he offered to adopt three of the more attractive (less mangey) cats.

I originally saw Malcolm as the most promising of the prospective tenants who had answered my advertisement: Unique large 2-room apartment (with turret), new bathroom and kitchen, heat included, access to shared washer and dryer. He arrived with one little hand held suitcase, and a pillow. He looked like an orphan out of a Dickens novel. But Malcolm, it turned out, was an extremely successful author (nom de plume: Annabel Maude Urquhart) of those steamy, salacious bodice-rippers that adorn book racks in airports, garage sales and supermarkets everywhere. He made absolutely no apology for his chosen genre; his royalty cheques arrived promptly and his bills were covered. "It pays me well with an abundance remaining," he told me. "I'm stashing away absolute sack-fuls," he chortled.

In the first year of his tenancy, when Hallowe'en season rolled around, he came downstairs for a chat. There are two stairwells in our old house, one being off the kitchen where I was currently sitting around the island when I heard the door from the attic open. When his happy face rounded the corner, I encountered "Maude" for the first time. Maude was Malcolm's alter-ego. She was a whimsical, slim little feather wearing a bobbed blond wig and enormous fluttering eyelashes. At the side of her kewpie doll mouth (boldly outlined in a murderous red) was a perfectly placed beauty mark.

"I know this is a shock for you. Please hear me out. I'm Maude when I "dress", he giggled. I have **such** a fetish for 30's era women's fashions and love to play fashionista." All of this he said in a breathy kind of way as he caught hold of the sides of his floral dress and dreamily circled the kitchen table while I sat with mouth agape.

"I sensed," he continued hesitantly in his best southern drawl, "even at the beginning, that you'd be understanding of the . . . unusual . . . or . . . the arcane . . .

or the eccentric . . . and wouldn't feel too uncomfortable when I "dress" . . . please . . . please, please be okay with this . . . it's still me under these frills. It's still me." And finally . . . "Say something."

"You look very pretty," I answered.

We continued on, the three of us, in a kind of weirdly off-kilter harmony. I would occasionally be reminded of Maude's presence when Malcolm needed the washer/drier and would descend to do laundry dressed in feather boas and extravagant silk robes. These appeared to be her favourite writing ensembles.

His female literary characters ranged from the downtrodden waif-turned-prostitute to the straight-laced Victorian heroine or the cowgirl or frontier gal or the 50's modern housewife. Maude's stories, set in various time periods, were often reworked themes from previous plots. Even she admitted, she rarely strayed from her proven formula: i.e. main character faces: unfathomable loss / harassment / difficult decision / missed opportunity / unexpected obstacle / deceitful legal counsel / scheming family members / lost pet / cataclysmic natural disaster / shocking health diagnosis . . . who needs . . . to fend off unwanted advances from neighbour / stalker / banker or . . . needs more confidence / money / appreciative husband / loyal wife / property / lost passport / better opportunity / improved status / respect / custody of children / the perfect wedding dress / release from prison / crash diet / to overcome fear of _____/ more friends /a better job etc.

Her writings had served her well and allowed for extravagant indulgences. Malcolm may have originally arrived with few belongings, however, that changed once he had taken up permanent residency. He had a passion for books and ordered crates of assorted genres from online sources. He then undertook to have the many needed bookcases constructed and proceeded to hire carpenters to have them permanently bolted in place throughout the attic. They spanned three walls of his main living area which held the kitchen/living room and bedroom areas. They stretched around this huge area ending on either side of the turret. He had chosen beautifully crafted cabinetry and let me know he considered these shelves as part of his investment into my restoration.

One Saturday morning, Maude (**not** an eschewer of shoes) took the attic stairs down to the kitchen when she knew I would be having morning coffee.

"I have a fabulous suggestion for making our . . . your house THE go-to destination for October 31."

"Share away," I answered. "Always pleased to hear a fabulous suggestion."

Malcolm's idea was a buzzer/intercom system which would notify him to trigger a pulley and cable system to release candy treats from his third floor turret. He said the genesis for this brainstorm came to him in a moment of wild inspiration.

"And If your house is to look properly haunted, let's go all out."

And go all out we did, or rather he/she did. Never has an adult more gleefully thrown themselves into such a project with such wild abandon. Our neighbourhood enjoyed a hugely popular Hallowe'en evening and Malcolm generously picked up the entire tab on everything. Kids and parents lined up on the sidewalk and burst out laughing every time the buzzer alerted him to flip on the turret lights and start his "Ghostly Gallows" show. Sometimes he would alternate this with an Adams' Family routine using large Morticia and Gomez cutout figures releasing the "Hand" in order to descend by pulley to bring the goodies down to the curbside. It was easy for me to admit that Malcolm had made my house the hit of the neighbourhood. Hallowe'en, for me, has now become what Malcolm has made it. He loves the pagan roots of Hallowe'en as a yearly finger to established religion. "Who can't love a celebration allowing men to dress up as women and women to dress up as sex objects?"

That Hallowe'en intercom system then expanded into an efficient method to accept his many home deliveries. A professionally installed alert system would be exceptionally useful for both of us, he said and I had to agree. An entry phone at the front gate would be connected to both apartments and would save us a lot of steps in identifying callers. This would allow the front gate to swing open and the delivery to be left at the front door. Very useful for an agoraphobe.

As someone who never ventured outside our four walls, Malcolm had an abundance of strange and exotic visitors. One group affected the same Art Nouveau dress code arriving in extravagant gowns and headgear. Then there was the group who performed pantomime. They would gather in Malcolm's attic to entertain each other wordlessly amidst loud and raucous hoots and hollerings. Then there were the puppeteers who would thump up and down the stairs carrying their wooden puppets in all shapes and sizes of suitcases. Sock puppetry followed. It seems Malcolm had located all his like-minded groups through Facebook. Some were weekend transvestites, some were adoring fans of the Marcel Marceau School of French Mime and some were just plain ordinary everyday folk who simply wanted to practice throwing their voices through puppets without moving their lips.

But my favorite Malcolm visitors were his older twin siblings, William and Gwendolyn (Wendy) plus their spouses and children. Sunday dinners in Malcolm's attic was the highlight of their week. After the big meal, they played board games or danced or entertained each other until it was past the childrens' bedtime. Then, in a loud and cranky explosion, they would descend the stair well through my kitchen to say a goodnight to me and a thank you for putting up with their noise.

Malcolm, as a small boy, was a compulsive daydreamer, a problematic fact he says for his teachers and a horror for his parents. As a young student, he found school frequently so boring that his only release was to drift off. During his middle school years, he fantasized constantly about being a cat, the domestic animal his mother most adored. While most pre-pubescent boys were dreaming of the lady lumps under the blouses of their female teachers, Malcolm was refining his "cat washes face" routine which he once used to entertain the largely ambivalent lunch room crowd. It was a completely mesmerizing moment until he let out a strangled "miaow" which seemed to break the spell. His audience had remained frozen in time during his pantomime, lunch trays in hand, and perhaps suddenly felt collectively foolish for being so entranced. Despite the fact that no one applauded, Malcolm saw how captivated they were. For that very brief moment he had the complete and undivided attention of the entire lunchroom and it was powerful. His kind and protective older twin siblings tried to break it to him gently that it was a particularly un-cool thing to do. Perhaps he should save these moments for family gatherings.

Malcolm, however remained undaunted and continued refining his mimicry, adding occasional voices and soon discovered ventriloquism. Now, he really had the attention of his classmates. They began to look to him to provide endless entertainment. When he was able to imitate the sound of the intercom being activated followed by the principal making an announcement, the teachers were at his mercy.

Watching someone like Malcolm who lived (occasionally as Maude) so entirely alone and happy has made me reassess my own decisions in that regard. As a child, I had no choice in the family into which I was born. It was a very small family unit: a widowed mother, domineering twin aunt, sly uncle, largely absent older brother, estranged extended family members who remained unknown to me for years. I realize, perhaps because of this, I have often filled my life with certain people who did not contribute to my well-being. But, at the time, I was probably needy . . . or lonely . . . or . . . restless. And then I think of Malcolm and I witness the gleeful wackiness that can exist for someone like him who lives so completely in his head and on his own. There seems to be no one else's company he enjoys quite so much as his own.

"You have so much fun in your life, Maude," I commented to her one Saturday morning. "You seem to keep yourself endlessly entertained."

"It's something I have to work at . . . endlessly," Maude answered quietly.

"But it all comes to you so readily," I countered. "You make me realize that I want more fun and laughter in my life."

"I think you're a bit over-tired this morning," she consoled. "Your weekends don't give you enough time to recharge in order to meet your students on Monday morning. This is how burn-out happens, dear friend."

"Seriously, Maude. Was it your upbringing that gives you this happy outlook? I imagine you had a loving and supportive family to be able to exude such . . . buoyancy."

"If I told you about my life, I mean . . . truthfully . . . really told you about the unsavoury parts of my upbringing, you'd be very surprised. Because I'm so buoyant, as you call it, you think it was like this for me from the start?"

"Maude, I'm not meaning to pry. I know we all have baggage. It's unlikely that everything in your past was a cakewalk. After all, you're gay and that's something I personally have never had to deal with."

"Wait right here," she said, "I want to show you something."

And with that, Maude clip-clopped back upstairs (in the highest of heels) and brought down her latest manuscript.

"This is how fantasy has helped me reshape my life," she said as the stack of pages was laid on the table before me. "I constantly re-imagine my life. Through all my writings, I create new scenarios that are rewarding and satisfying. If I can live in my imagination I can somehow soften all the sharp corners of my childhood and keep out the shadowy thoughts that menace my peace of mind.

FUNNY BONE (AND ITS GLOSSARY OF TERMS) ANNABEL MAUDE URQUART

At the time we meet Maude Pickles, she has lived through two decades of name calling aimed at her family. Because of their surname*, Maude's family is often a target. It doesn't help that her brother had been named Dilbert. "Dilly" Pickles? Seriously? Had no one made mention of this questionable choice to the parents? Dilbert's twin sister was named "Olive". Again . . . ?

Maude's family has affectionate nicknames for each other which has further bonded them against the rude barbs* from the outside world. Maude is called "Silly Pickles" for years because she is such a flibbertigibbet*. Later, as a teenager, her nickname became "Sour". The general moodiness of adolescence* inspires that little bit of ridicule, thank you very much. Understandably, for Maude, those were memories over which she is both happy yet conflicted. Maude finally realizes her family is quite unique and their questionable sense of humour is indeed delightful. She knows leaving home will rob her of that great joy and so, she plans to stay with her family for a long, long time.

Maude has had the good fortune to have a very loving upbringing. She has been blessed with parents who are still in love after twenty-five years plus two older siblings, twelve years older than Maude. Her twin brother and sister still live at home. In fact, one of Maude's strongest memories is being escorted to school on her very first day by her two older siblings, Dil on one side and Olie on the other. They both held her hands.

Maude had come as a great surprise to her parents who were quite sure they were finished with child rearing.

"This newly arrived little bundle is SO very different from the twins," says Maude's mother as she gazes wistfully into baby Maude's crib.

"I completely agree," answered Mr. Pickles, "so, so-o-o different. After all, there's only one of her."

Maude's older brother and sister had always been entirely wrapped up in each other, inside and outside of the womb*. In fact, the parents felt oddly peripheral*in the upbringing of their two older children. The twins had private twin games and secret twin signals and a strange twin language which they used long into their adult lives. Both twins now still lived at home and helped with the family business.

Maude's parents run a Bouncy House business out of their garage. It started years ago when they sold helium filled balloons, party favours, silly string and streamers. But it really took off (har-de-har) when they added bouncy castles and later, trampolines. The openings of their Trampoline and Foam Pits Parks (Pickles Park 1and 2) have been great successes.

Every kid in the neighbourhood wanted to visit the Pickles' house. Father had installed a circular slide from the upper floors into the kitchen by removing an old servant's stairwell. The acceleration gained from the third floor turret level was considerable and always elicited a panicked cry of "LOOK OUT BELOW" before a very rude thump ended onto the pantry floor.

Dillie and the girls soon perfected their own style of an elegant slide exit. It consisted of "sticking" the landing onto two firmly planted stable feet, shoulder width apart. A small hesitation to gain balance followed, and then, with feet together, an erect and Olympic-worthy arched back plus a casual skippity-hop stroll to the fridge finished the entire execution. They all agreed it was a thing of great beauty.

Maude, growing up, had her own idiosyncrasies* which were quite different from the rest of the family. As a toddler with unformed speech, she often appeared to be having lengthy conversations with imaginary friends. Those same imaginary friends rode on the back of her tricycle or played trucks with her in the sandbox. Sometimes they sat around her play table for tea parties with her teddy bears. When she played dress up, if they didn't cooperate, she would scold them and send them to bed.

Maude began to mispronounce words which the family found adorable. So words like "breftis" for "breakfast" or "upsighted" for "upset" or "bezhausted" for "exhausted" or "oftis" for "office" became the lingua franca* of the household. Words were frequently "Maude-ified" to illustrate how far the joke could be pushed. A constant attempt was made to out-pun each other. Visitors to the Pickles household were uniformly subjected to all this eye-rolling humour.

As a child at school, Maude surprised her teachers with detailed descriptions of the colours in numbers and alphabet *letters. Certain words were great favourites because of their colour combinations. Maude was especially fond of any word containing an "x" because of its bright purple hue. Her own name was playfully scrawled across many notebook pages just to watch the oranges and pinks unfurl like a flag.*

Maude could even see auras* surrounding people. Sometimes angry adults had ugly shades of dark blackish-green around their entire bodies.

"I need to completely avoid those people," she said to one of her imaginary* friends.

Her own family was always surrounded with auras of a bright canary yellow. Sometimes it was a paler yellow, but they were always filled with light.

As Maude grew older, she became increasingly aware of her special powers. She began to feel messages being directed toward her. She once heard a dog tell her about his tight collar, so she loosened it. The happy smile on the dog's face was unmistakable.

"So, now I speak Dog?" she said to no one in particular. "This is toe-riffic!"

She soon realized a great affinity* for the natural world, our Maude did. She had often felt the trees talking to her, especially when a wind storm was brewing. And, periodically, the thoughts of others crept into her brain. Random words would scroll in front of her eyes as she stood in line for grocery store checkouts or bank teller line ups. Whose words was she receiving? She felt they were simply unresolved anxieties floating about in her immediate vicinity and she was the receptor.

"Hey, Trudy?" implored one message, "How are the crops this year?"

Maude turned to the woman standing behind her and said, "Trudy? . . . "I'm hearing a voice asking me about your harvest. Are you able to get the wheat in before the snow flies?

It wasn't long before Maude's perceptive abilities came to the attention of the local media. Over the next two years, she gained considerable notoriety*. Maude helped families understand their unruly pets. She visited zoos to help with difficult animal births. She coaxed cats out of trees.

Some of her best work involved helping stroke victims communicate with their families. One elderly stroke patient who had fancied himself a stand-up comedian appreciated her as the audience he had lost by telling her one joke after another. His daily, identical set list began with a series of knock-knock jokes followed by,

"So, a _____walks into a bar." This was all done telepathically* but Maude still laughed out loud.

Maude, who had grown up in a household in which any attempt at comedy was richly rewarded, realized how vital it is to promote laughter. She was very satisfied helping others but felt her own life lacked the humour and joy she knew was personally essential.

At twenty-one, she was set up on a blind date by her older sister. Olive felt Maude needed to experience more of life.

"Enough with all these canines and felines and geriatrics, Maude. You need to meet someone your own age who is not covered in fur," coaxed Olive. "You'll like him, I think."

When Maude phoned Olive the next day to recount the evening, she began with her date's most annoying habit. He had taken Maude out to dinner.

"How can I take anyone seriously who audibly itemizes everything on the menu including the price? Does he think I'm illiterate and can't read?"

"Maude, he might not have heard of your psychic reputation."

"So, in this instance, that must mean what, exactly?" Maude replied.

*"H-mmm-m-m-m-m. Maybe, you just **heard** him thinking," mumbled Olive. "This probably wasn't the greatest idea," she added quietly.*

But actually, it turned out to be . . . not a bad idea at all. Olive had given her sister the insightful tool of actually using her skills in reading someone else's mind to enable relationships. The ramifications were staggering. She began to see her telepathic abilities branching out into the many areas of relationship counselling. And with any luck, she could assist those unions in remaining humorous and light-hearted.

But, three months later, after a series of failed attempts to patch together couples on the verge of divorce, Maude reluctantly acknowledged her skills lay in her own intuitive powers and not in her ability to encourage compromise between the genders* When her clients realized she could actually read their minds, they became hostile to being held so completely accountable. Maude's last therapy session ended violently when a wife related a conversation she frequently had with her husband. They told Maude they were promising complete and total honesty from each other. The wife said she had looked at her husband and asked, "Do these pants make me look fat?" Maude had read the husband's mind when he hesitated before he answered, "Of course not, my love.". It was at this point that Maude interjected with a reminder that this WAS about telling the truth, wasn't it? The violence which followed wasn't directed against the husband by his angry wife or against the wife by her embarrassed husband. In this instance it was the husband whose fist was directed at Maude who escaped a sound thrashing by nimbly positioning herself out of his reach.

That evening, feeling completely defeated, she made her way home through her neighbourhood park. Passing by a duck pond, she heard a voice call out, "Hey there! Got bread? Got popcorn?"

It was a duck. A male mallard duck. After he and Maude exchanged introductory pleasantries, Harvey the Duck felt he had found a kindred spirit. He waddled out of the pond on his big flat, orange duck feet, shook off his feathers and followed Maude down the road.

Harvey, scientific name . . . *Anas platyrhynchos* . . . had brown and black feathers atop a smooth taupe coloured body. Around his neck was a little white band of feathers like a small starched Edwardian collar. Other than his fluorescent green head and yellow bill, he was a species perfectly blended for environmental camouflage.

His lady friend, Audrey, watched his exit from the pond with interest. Harvey turned back to the pond and nodded for her to join him. Audrey gracefully exited the water, smoothed her little brown tweed jacket and delicately shook her tail feathers. She happily followed Harvey, who was happily following Maude.

The Pickles household was overjoyed to welcome Harvey and Audrey. Mrs. Pickles immediately filled a bathtub for their new family pets. Dilbert and Olive went online to find a nutritious food source for Harvey and his mate. And, no, it wasn't "quackers" (Mr. Pickles was especially proud of that one).

Maude began to incorporate Harvey and Audrey into her visits to seniors in residential care. The two ducks were a great hit with everyone and when Maude began to pick up rescue dogs and cats to add to their visitations, Harvey made the group harmonious*. Animal tricks became their much admired entertainment and were greeted with lengthy, appreciative applause. (Maude had neglected to consider the fact that her three rescue dogs were **not** of uniform size. However, more about that later).

When they went visiting, Harvey and Audrey rode along on the backs of two of the dogs. Leashes were not needed but Maude complied with municipal rules and all mammals were harnessed. Compostable bags for the dogs' poop were always used responsibly. Maude rode her bike (pink with orange handlebar streamers) with the two cats up front in the wicker basket. Maude's pink and orange helmet matched her bike.

Maude always gave instructions to Harvey who in turn passed them on to the group. Their presentation began with all three dogs (Alfie, Winston and Frankie), the two cats (both named Elizabeth) and then the two ducks sitting in a row on their haunches, smiling. (Frankie was always reluctant to "haunch" because she said it made her look fat). Tails would thump on the floor, cats would purr and Harvey and Audrey would quack in unison.

Maude had sewn little matching jackets and hats for her many animals. At Easter, their hats all had floppy bunny ears.

Then, led by Harvey and Audrey, the line of animals would walk around the room, in between all the tables and chairs, much to the delight of their audience. Maude would follow at the end of the line, accompanying them on her kazoo, playing a selection of polka tunes. The Polish Wedding March was always a great favourite.

Their signature performance piece was an animal pyramid: three dogs on the bottom, then the two cats formed the second tier and finally, Harvey and Audrey formed the crown. It was a highly asymmetrical pyramid, however, because of the different dog sizes, but happily all the animals made it work beautifully.

Sometimes, when Audrey felt particularly aerobatic, she would stand on one bright orange duck foot and happily quack while wing-flapping.

In all of her life, Maude had never known such complete fulfillment and total happiness. Self-acceptance, she determined, is a wonderful gift.

A GLOSSARY OF TERMS FOR FUNNY BONE
In A Very Imprecise Alphabetical Order

1. **Asymmetrical:** *off-balanced, frequently what happens when you cut your own hair*
2. **Adolescence:** *an unfortunate teenage gap marked by splotchy facial complexion problems*
3. **Surname:** *your family name, e.g. "Pickles" is Maude's surname. Her family name (as determined by Ancestory. com) comes from the Polish surname "Ogorki" meaning "pickles"; hence, Polski Ogorki, a well established European condiment producer.*

4. **Barbs**: *slings and arrows of outrageous fortune (Hamlet, Act III, Scene I)*

5. **Flibbertigibbet:** *a fuzzy and imprecise thinker, a marcher to her own drumbeat*

6. **Idiosyncrasies:** *wonderfully eccentric and off-beat quirkinesses displayed by an individual outside the mainstream of acceptance*

7. **Aura:** *that glow-y halo of light surrounding the object or person viewed*

8. **Affinity:** *drawn irrevocably toward something; sort of like your tongue to a frozen post in winter*

9. **Peripheral:** *outside of; like trying to find the pass code into an exclusive membership*

10. **Geriatrics:** *older, lovely people who always want to slip you money*

11. **Womb:** *a quiet, hidden place inside a mother's body where her baby grows*

12. **Harmonious:** *congenial, not to be confused with harmonica which is an instrument used by Bob Dylan (noted poet and Nobel winner for Literature)*

13. **Notoriety:** *your reputation as embarrassingly disclosed on social media*

14. **Intuition**: *that weird little internal voice that tells you stuff*

15. **Telepathically:** *the ability to hear the phone before it starts to ring*

16. **Lingua franca:** *a language everyone uses; street lingo e.g. "aks" instead of "ask"*

17. **Haunches:** *bum bones*

18. **Fluorescent:** *extre-e-e-emely bright*

19. Gender: *now defined as male/female/L/G/B/T/Q/duck/dog/cat*

20. Kindred: *like-minded; same-same; Maude likes to think it means fear of relatives.*

JOKES WHICH MAUDE THINKS YOU MIGHT LIKE: (She did not make these up.)

1. *Outside a dog, a man's best friend is a book.*
   Inside a dog, it's very dark.
2. *Clones are people two.*
3. *A horse walks into a bar and the bartender asks, "Why the long face?" (This may be Maude's all-time favourite.)*
4. *A day without sunshine is . . . like, night.*
5. *PMS: Pardon My Screaming.*

When I finished reading, I looked up to see Maude with tears in her eyes.

"Maude," I asked hesitantly, "why the tears? . . . Why are you upset?

"My family . . . my parents . . . the love and support you think I grew up with didn't come from my parents. They came from my brother and sister, not my parents. My mother and father were alcoholics. Homophobic, mean-spirited, brutally judgemental . . . a torment. When I finally came out to them at fifteen, they asked me to leave home immediately. Actually, they threw me out that very night. If it had not been for my older siblings, I may have ended up on the street. This is how I've rewritten my upbringing. I couldn't withstand any more ugly words from the mouths of my mother and father; they both had a neurotic fear of homosexuality. I knew even as a small child . . . all their horrid words. They also took out their drunken rages against each other on me. My brother and sister rescued me after I was abandoned. William and Wendy couldn't bear to see what was happening. **They** are my family, my **true** family. Not my parents.

My abusive father died about 20 years ago and my mother locked herself up in . . . our old stone house and lived alone with her cats until she needed to be placed in a care-home for Alzheimer's patients.

And then . . . you came along, and bought my childhood home. You . . . you bought my parents' old ramshackled mansion.

You've lovingly put your heart into its refurbishment and I feel I owe you a great deal. This decade with you has allowed me to rewrite my life surrounded by love and laughter. Annabel Maude Urquhart and I have had another chance to live a new life here with you."

14

WWW.MATCH.COM

When New Year 2000 commences without the anticipated Y2K disaster, all international markets breathe a huge sigh of relief. The world's industries go back to business as usual. The turning of the century marks the first publication of a comic strip cartoon by an artist named Charles Schultz and the most popular song is by Faith Hill. Using the internet to connect romantically is a fairly new practice.

Today we find Alice, at her computer, scanning the personal profiles on **www.match.com**. She is similar to scores of women her age who find the allure of online dating equally scandalous and happily opportunistic. She reads a particular personal ad with interest:

TALL, FIT, ATTRACTIVE GENTLEMAN, 65, SEEKS WOMAN AGED 50 - 55, EQUALLY FIT, ACTIVE, WHO APPRECIATES A RANGE OF ACTIVITIES FROM THE SYMPHONY TO WESTERN

LINE DANCING. MUST BE FINANCIALLY INDEPENDENT AND WILLING TO TRAVEL.
ABSOLUTELY NO EMOTIONAL BAGGAGE, PLEASE.

She reads this online profile from Lars36 with the critical eye as to what has been highlighted.

It is always said of Lars that he presents well. He is tall with an overly confident air which many see as arrogant. That confidence serves him well in entering online dating at the age of 65.

Typically, for someone of Lars's generation, he has absolutely no computer knowledge. He is at a distinct disadvantage. Even keyboarding is outside his skillset. But Lars meets a group of loners through the Wallflower Singles Dinner Club who show him the fundamentals and soon, ***www.match.com*** becomes his ticket to meeting women. At this time, online dating is a growing curiosity and novelty. It is a practice which is deemed a sure sign of desperation. Catfishing is a relatively unknown phenomenon and to meet someone online is NOT acknowledged as mainstream.

Lars knows he has a great advantage on these dating websites. Most men in his age category don't even have a full head of hair! Lars has developed a few smooth moves during the course of his six and a half decades which have provided him a constant string of women after he left his short marriage forty years ago.

He's the kind of man who has never fully understood the difficulties some men have in being successful with women. Women are easy; it's the relationships which are the toe-stubbers. He has found women to be the best listeners, the most accepting of his excuses, very forgiving, the best audience for his grandstanding, always willing to split expenses and endlessly appreciative of his eagerness to cook.

At first, the fellas from the Dinner Club view Lars in a friendly way but soon grow cautious. Initially they feel confident in welcoming this handsome stranger into their dinner group but are quick to realize Lars is not a team player. He is entirely for himself and sees no advantage in fostering male friendships. If only the dinner club fellas knew of Lars's basic insecurities, they may have felt less shunned or discarded when they weren't needed anymore to prop him up socially. No one knows of his obsession with scouring the phone directories from North America's major cities to find relatives with his own unusual surname. Surely there's someone out there who is a distant relative. How was it his mother had left the two of them so isolated?

Lars grew up in post-WWII, into a set of circumstances he alternately denies and embellishes. He exaggerates his parentage because he has never known his father. He fantasizes about a big, muscular man (like himself) who had met his mother before she became grossly "enlarged" and eventually slovenly.

As a teenager, life with his mother was tough. She cleaned apartments and private homes. She expanded her cleaning into business centers and shopping malls which usually meant night shifts with Lars being left unsupervised. He grew to resent the demands of being alone in their poorly furnished rooming house in a rough area of downtown Toronto. Those feelings of abandonment were compounded by what he saw on the streets when he took to wandering out on his own. Even the hookers were too aggressive. Once he remembers witnessing a knifing; a trauma for a young child to witness. When he informed his mother he was leaving school at the end of Grade VII in order to help her with money, she was both touched by his heartfelt sympathies and ashamed of the lack of opportunities she needed to provide. However, it was 1953 and the Canadian government could not enforce public education past twelve years of age.

Despite an education cut short, Lars possesses the intellectual goods to be a thinker. He has also become a heightened observer. Lars assesses every motive, every hesitation, every nuanced response in every encounter. He has begun to fashion elaborate explanations for the many disappointing and shameful aspects of his life. He explains his poverty-strewn upbringing as a sad rejection of his then teenage mother from her *supposedly* wealthy east coast family. He hides his lack of education by stocking his personal library with impressive titles. Now, at 65, since he still needs to work to provide income, his explanation for lack of money is explained as mismanagement by imaginary business partners. Lars lives on pension money plus weekly paychecks from his part time employment at hardware stores or lumber yards. He lives in a fifth-wheel in a trailer park which he feels gives him the illusion of a gypsy-ish lifestyle. His seemingly vagabond attitude to the impermanence of roots he passes off as a nod to romance. His money has gone into creating the appearance of wealth. His closet contains designer fashions purchased from vintage boutiques. His high-end shoes are kept polished with inserts to maintain their shapes. His coats and sweaters are cashmere.

Growing up with only his mother has left Lars with a lifelong dread of holiday celebrations. When he was 25, he met a beautiful girl from a large Italian family. Their imminent marriage briefly provided him with happy family experiences. For Lars, there were actual moments of real camaraderie with his fiance's siblings. Soon, however, his three future brothers-in-law quickly saw through the polished veneer to his mean-spirited core. They warned their sister against going ahead with her wedding, but to no avail. Prior to the ceremony, many of the wedding guests inquired as to why no one had ever met any of Lars's family. They are unaware of how he keeps his obesely diabetic mother firmly closeted.

Intensely jealous of the camaraderie the three brothers shared with his bride's father, Lars made a seriously ill-conceived wedding speech which was originally intended to honor his new bride. His five minutes of microphone time was used to belittle and mock her Italian family for their quaint ethnic habits. He actually thought his delivery was impeccable and its contents humorous. Needless to say, his new bride was left feeling betrayed and totally mortified. It did not help that Lars had no one from his family in attendance at the wedding. (The brothers had only begrudgingly agreed to serve as attendants). So, after that tragic wedding speech, they began to climb over each other in an attempt to pummel Lars's face.

Newly married, his bride repeatedly encounters his intolerance for compromise of any sort. As their many arguments occur, he does not see his stubbornness as a serious shortcoming. He has made his own decisions since he was twelve and knows obstinately that **his** way is the **only** way. His lack of introspection has left him judgemental and intransigent. Further conversation of any of his questionable behaviors is a mental torture for him. In such instances he is able only to withdraw abruptly and slam any available door. After his new young bride arranges for an intervention by the priest from her parish, Lars moves into his own apartment and eventually files for a separation agreement. Because of her religion, divorce is out of the question. For Lars, it serves as a reminder of the underlying true nature of women in general.

Forty trips around the sun later, after four decades of dozens of discarded relationships, we find Lars discovering the wealth of dating possibilities on his chosen website. He has moved steadily westward across Canada toward the coast of British Columbia and finally settles on Vancouver Island. Further travel west would involve crossing an ocean. (This thought causes him to resurrect a memory of an advertisement for travel as a professional escort on single cruises. A tuxedo is needed. He stores that away for future reference.)

His travel west (he tells others) is to avoid harsh prairie winters which is partly true. However, we know it's often to escape the fallout from broken relationships as well as financial involvements in failed investment schemes.

In Victoria, the DinnerClub men whom Lars briefly milked for computer knowledge have all fallen away due mainly to his neglect. However, his ruggedly handsome looks continue to give him an advantage which he flaunts indecently. He has maintained a flat stomach with all the recommended core exercises. The thrice weekly gym visits provide Lars with a handy selection of seemingly impressionable women plus the constant motivation to maintain a toned physique. For him, the only two flies-in-the-ointment are (1) his left ear hearing loss due to a failing cochlear connection (a final genetic gift from his long dead diabetic mother) and (2) the beginning signs of a problematic prostate.

In response to Alice's indication of "interest", Lars36 is eager to read Alice's profile:

ATTRACTIVE, ACTIVE, 5' 7", OUTDOORSY 55 YR. OLD WOMAN SEEKS GENTLEMAN FOR DAY-HIKING, TRAVELING, FINE DINING AND MAYBE . . . GOLD-PANNING? I'M ARTISTIC, CURIOUS, CONVERSATIONAL AND SPONTANEOUS.

It is always said of Alice that she presents well. She is tall-ish with a lithe, athletic build. She gives off a confident, easy-going air which inspires strangers to find her humorous and trustworthy.

Alice grew up in the household of a widowed mother alongside one older brother. Alice's mother was a twin and when the husband of her mother's twin showed an unusual and questionable interest in little five-year old Alice, the decision to place Alice in a convent during the school week was an easy solution. Alice's mother and her twin sister had themselves been raised in convents and therefore felt the "Good Sisters" would provide the necessary nurturing environment. Despite being a non-Catholic, Alice's mother knew the nuns would ensure a safe, supervised haven during the school week.

When she was growing up, Alice had agonized over her adolescent face. Some days she had parted her hair on the right; other days, she was inclined to part on the left. This "hair part thing" stemmed, she figured, from her many childhood and young adolescent convent years when she really never knew her reflection. Convents are renowned for their dearth of mirrors. Thank you, Good Sisters, for your misplaced noble intentions to curb vanity. Reflections in glass cabinet doors and windows had been what Alice had come to rely on for a sense of what she looked like. Every weekend upon her return home from her weekly stay at the convent, Alice would tread a constant and incessant path into worn linoleum between the small mirrors in her mother's house. Her wild and curly hair was like nothing she could control. She recalled a cringe-worthy memory of the nuns inflicting an atrocious red bow for a class photo.

Alice still carries an enduring sense of the rigid rules the Good Sisters imposed for personal hygiene. A small tag printed with "36" had been sewn into all of Alice's clothes. For her years at the convent, she was number 36. Convent laundries and the sorting of clothing relied on this system for redistribution. Inside all those scratchy wool stockings, navy-blue tunics, white blouses with both short and long sleeves, garter belts, nightgowns, underwear, cardigans and coats, the inevitable number 36. That the number 36 tag was also sewn onto the collar of a nightgown to be worn into the tub on bath night was something she questioned reluctantly.

The convent bathroom was immense to Alice's young eyes. No mirrors, two double-sided rows of sinks in the middle of a pale yellow tiled room with bath cubicles along the four walls. Two chairs for the supervising nuns were placed in opposite corners. Alice was directed into one of the doorless bath cubicles and told to crouch into a near scalding three inches of water. She was then instructed to wash her body from underneath her bath nightgown. Even though convents were always chilly, the nuns told her totally immersing a body would have been wasteful.

Alice would remember being returned to the convent every Sunday evening after her weekends at home. She recalled an early photo of herself standing on the convent steps, wearing her little dark navy uniform with a white blouse. One black knee-high down around her ankle. Large glasses framed timid eyes.

Upon re-entry through the front doors of this imposing gothic structure, a bell-ring-and-nun-sentry-door bolt was released. Alice would then walk through lengthy brown corridors, on heavily waxed brown linoleum, past rows of nuns' black bicycles, past wood-lined niches containing chipped alabaster statues of bleeding-heart saints, up narrow stairwells to her dormitory with her assigned bed and washstand.

Her deeply seated feelings of anger accumulated over the course of her convent years. From such things as the threat of a nun's swinging rosary belt against her legs if multiplication tables weren't repeated quickly enough . . . from a dining hall incident where she was made to continue sitting in front of her regurgitated lump-filled rice pudding . . . from the severe corporal punishments and noticeable discriminations meted out against her First Nations playmates for such disrespectful acts as giggling during prayers or speaking their native tongue . . . from being made to watch while the nuns administered these beatings.

Once, as her punishment for an infraction (shoplifting, she thinks), Alice's mother prevented her from coming home for her usual weekend visit. Alice was so enraged by this loss of privilege that upon hearing this news, she rushed toward an upright piano situated on a raised platform and somehow managed to push it off the edge. Falling and landing on its back was enough to entirely dismantle most of this enormous instrument which clanged and crashed and clanged and crashed. Alice remembers herself lifting up toward the ceiling. She was now able to look down on the scene beneath her. And from this elevation, Alice can see her own little red-faced self, fists clenched, facing a trio of silent, frightened nuns.

As Alice matures into womanhood, she fosters quirky personal habits to convey a quick-witted humor to cover up pain. She always reads a magazine back-to-front, likes to eat pumpkin pie with her hands and once tries to sweeten her coffee with a jellybean. She has given up attempting to cook, acknowledging her only affinity for the kitchen is coordinating the table linens to the dinner ware.

But, Lars and Alice are not privy to any part of these significant backstories when they read each other's profiles on *www.match.com*. Tonight as we watch Lars and Alice greet each other for the first time, we see their smiling faces reflected in the subtle restaurant lighting. We know they are bringing their most dynamic selves to this first meeting. Dressed in their best manners, they are alert to any red flags while appearing happily conversational. There is neither the slightest indication of Lars's narcissism nor Alice's deep-seated anger. No emotional baggage is allowed to appear. They will begin to tell their stories and laugh at each other's humorous anecdotes. They will delight in what they have in common. In time, both will be slow to acknowledge that what they fundamentally share is a neurotic fear of engulfment alongside a horror of abandonment.

15

A FORK IN THE EYE

Based loosely on the 2011 Alberta judicial ruling of a battered wife who was sentenced to 18 years in prison for the murder of her abusive husband. After lengthy negotiations between the Crown and her lawyer, she pleaded guilty to manslaughter. Her term was reduced after three years on appeal and she was released under strict supervision.

I, _____ am the court appointed therapist following her discharge from prison. At 58, she has been released into a designated halfway house. One of her day parole requirements is weekly counseling sessions as part of her conditional manslaughter sentence for first degree murder resulting from domestic abuse.

SESSION NOTES:
1) Monday, April 5, 2014

She had grown up with few parental influences. Her personal life choices received almost no scrutiny from a caring adult. Her sweet mother had died early, leaving her with an odd childhood memory of the two of them quilting and taking straight pins out of a tomato shaped red pincushion with an attached dangling red strawberry. She had no one close to her other than her mother's sister who was only too happy to see her niece move out after highschool graduation.

In the intervening years between Grade XII and marriage, she had worked a string of low-entry jobs. Remarkably, she had always lived alone with the exception of a cat or two and kept almost completely to herself. She had been an exceptionally shy and vulnerable adolescent, easily swayed and trusting. She had grown into an equally shy and trusting adult. She had never travelled outside her home province.

She was 32 when she took a late shift working behind the bar at The CrossRoads and met this cute roughneck from the oil rigs. He was 25 and handsomely buffed. He seemed like a gentleman and tipped her generously. He saw quickly what a sweetheart she was. All her coworkers described her as such. Working the bar was lucrative but her chances for wholesome social connection were slim. It was mainly a venue for after work riggers and truckers, many of whom hid their wedding rings discreetly in blue jean pockets.

She had been slow to recognize his early abusive signs as such. It had started innocently as silly jibes, she recalled. They were just getting to know each other; there was lots of healthy verbal sparring. If it had stayed like that, as innocent jibes, she would have probably accepted it as simply his kind of put-down humour. She was older by only seven years, but that age difference became his constant source of a "dig" that went something like . . . "At your age . . . yuh know . . . well, chances grow slimmer for you to attract attention, haha" . . . or . . . "Better catch me while you are still physically capable, haha" She began to notice it was his constant go-to kind of comment. He frequently made these kinds of personal observations as a kind of jokey joke to passively slam her appearance or their age difference. He seemed to get juice by slyly criticizing her frailties or achievements. It occurred to her that perhaps this was a sign of his own inadequacies. She failed to see this as a red flag.

There was no one who helped her question herself in choosing him as a suitable husband. She never met any of his friends. He said he had no family; put into foster care early. Highschool dropout. Criminal record? Work history? Any trouble with drugs or alcohol? She asked none of these questions.

SESSION NOTES
2) Monday, April 12, 2014

Violent incidents over 25 of the 27 years of marriage. She related many examples calmly. Good level of recall. Retrieved incidental details and dates easily. Strong visual memory e.g. the horror on her boys' faces as they witnessed one particular beating. She recalled the colour of their matching t-shirts (and that they both needed a haircut) as they knelt beside her while she cradled her pregnant belly.

She remembered the rose coloured flocked wallpaper in their bedroom and her blood stains smeared on its floral pattern from another beating.

No doubt that she and her boys have suffered extensively from traumas at the hands of a man she would eventually murder.

(tape recording)

"I began to call them my "fork in the eye" moments. He threw a carton of milk at me once and it splattered across my chest. The boys were little at the time and it set all of 'em to howlin'. Then . . . he just left. Slammed the back door hard. Peeled outta the driveway with the car fish-tailin' and sprayin' gravel. I just knelt down on the linoleum right there, sopping up the milk mess, too stunned to even cry myself. Yeah . . . a definite fork in the eye moment.

"My god, that's horrible . . . Why "fork in the eye?" Tell me what that means to you."

"The first time I thought that way was the time he threw a dirty fork back at me. Had food still stuck on it, I guess. Hit me hard, square in the middle of my back. I was standing at the kitchen sink filling his water glass. He had come home for lunch and I could tell by his eyes that he seemed more agitated than usual. Always had to serve him as soon as he came through the door. So, when he picked up his fork, I guess he saw it wasn't clean. Maybe something at work had set him off . . . but food still stuck on a utensil was just too much it seems. He screamed a string of profane words while he thumped the table with his fists and then hurled the dirty fork at my back. I remember just standing still, quite frozen, my back toward him. I kept staring out the window over the sink watching the boys kicking a soccer ball in the backyard.

". . . what happened then?"

"I really don't remember much more. Not sure how long I stood just staring at the boys playin'. When I finally turned around, he wasn't there. Strangest thing. He wasn't at the table. He'd eaten the lasagne because his plate was empty. Car was gone too. I don't even remember hearing him leave. I looked down at the dirty fork still laying on the floor and when I picked it up, I held it in my closed fist and began to fantasize driving it into one of his eyes.

"The fork made you feel . . .?

"Brave."

"Would you say that was the first time you felt like fighting back?

"You mean, inflicting pain? Like actually making him feel actual pain? No, that wasn't the first time. But maybe it was the first time I let myself **really** feel it. The boys were little, the youngest only a toddler. I kinda scared myself thinking these violent thoughts. And the little boys were so . . . little."

"How long at this point had you been married?"

"Let's see. The oldest was six so we'd been married for about 7 years. He wasn't happy when I kept gettin' pregnant and by the time I was pregnant with our third, and the doctor said it was another boy, he was angry every time he looked at me. Said it was my fault. Wanted a girl."

(end of taping)

She said all this while gazing out my office window off to her right. She could have just as easily been describing the cloud shapes which held her attention.

SESSION NOTES
3) April 17

After a decade, she said she knew her husband realized she was becoming bolder. She periodically refused to continue with the isolation he imposed on their remote farm. The local school board became involved after it was made clear the boys were not being home schooled. Neighbors, store keepers and previous workplace friends began to report suspected domestic violence. One day he lost control in the middle of a grocery store. He had always been careful to contain his tirades to the privacy of their farm but this time there were others who witnessed his out of control temper. As he raged at her, yelling, "You fucking idiot!" he pulled open the glass doors of the frozen food lockers and began throwing bags of frozen vegetables directly at her head. He then turned toward the first exit he could find and stumbled erratically toward the parking lot. This was all caught on security cameras. She and her boys helped the supermarket workers pick up the mess. The store manager had intervened when he heard the shouting and reported this incident to the authorities. This resulted in her and the boys moving to a battered women's shelter for six months.

Seeking counselling at this point made her question the advice she could receive from the court-appointed professionals.

"You are demonstrating a kind of learned helplessness," offered one counselor.

"Stay down after you're hit," offered another.

Her husband then served a court imposed Restraining Order for Harassment with Assault and Battery. His sentence was for 6 months while she and her boys lived in the shelter. He received counselling for violent domestic abuse plus two years conditional supervised visitation privileges. He was reunited with his family at the end of the 6 months and they resumed living on their farm for the following decade.

SESSION NOTES:
4) Monday, April 24

During the three years after the family had been reunited, an integrated approach involving social services provided support. As a family they all received regular counselling. In the husband's case, he was required to take responsibility for his actions through constant monitoring and supervision. He was placed on strict probation and needed to report weekly to a parole officer. The justice system was eventually satisfied with his progress and felt confident there would be no risk for recidivism.

(tape recording)

"Tell me about your family life after reuniting with your husband."

"After we moved back to the farm, our life was calmer. His angry moods were less frequent. The triggers which used to send him over the edge seemed to have disappeared. He was less sullen and had even made some friends through counselling.

The boys were now seventeen, fifteen and twelve. Even they were less afraid of him although they were still very wary of his moods. They were always watchful. My boys had become extremely protective of me and he knew, deep down I think, that the four of us stood against him if it ever came to that. They were tall boys now . . . and muscular. He knew he couldn't take on the three of them. And they stood together, the boys.

"How about the immediate circumstances leading up to his death?"

The night I shot him, he came home late. I smelled the liquor on him; he'd been drinking heavily which was against his probation but I knew not to say anything. When he entered through the back door, he tripped over the hockey bags containing all the new hockey equipment that had been donated by the Kiwanis Club. It was worth hundreds and hundreds of dollars and all completely brand new. The boys were ecstatic and had gone to bed the happiest I had ever seen them. He was enraged and began to kick the equipment around the kitchen, yelling profanities. Then, he grabbed a butcher knife and began cutting and slashing the skates and jerseys. Finally, he dropped the knife and started kicking and hitting me in the stomach and face. Knocked out one of my front teeth. Blood everywhere. Then he staggered toward the staircase and stumbled his way up from the kitchen. I was afraid he'd drag the boys out of their beds and start whalin' on them. But when I followed him upstairs, he'd gone into our room and immediately passed out on the bed. I remember standing over him, holding a tea towel against my mouth, looking down on his stupid drunken gaping face. I knew right then he was unchanged. It was like all the months of counselling and intervention hadn't even happened. We would always, *always,* be living in a war zone. Nothing was different. One of our counsellors had told me that my boys feared daily for my life at the hands of their father.

That . . . that . . . was when I walked around to his side of the bed and got the loaded rifle he kept underneath . . . and I shot him . . . laid the barrel against his temple and . . . just pulled the trigger.

My oldest boy woke up when he heard the rifle shot. He found me sitting on the floor of our bedroom, holding the rifle and his dad on the bed with a bullet through his skull. We didn't talk about what had happened . . . right then. He helped me downstairs and we made a pot of coffee and talked about what to do. I was shaking pretty bad but I wasn't crying. We went back upstairs and wrapped his body in a shower curtain. Then we got a big metal container from the garage and dragged it into the kitchen to put his body in it. The bed was covered in blood and the room smelled of the rifle blast. We spent the night cleaning up the blood splatters and washing the floor. We burned all the bedding. The next morning, we drove the truck with the metal container and the bloody mattress out to a swampy part of our farm and dug a big hole. We had previously rented a backhoe to dig a new well so we used it to dig a bigger hole to bury the truck and the gun and all of his clothes. Our story for the social workers and the police was going to be . . .

that he had left a few evenings back and we hadn't seen him for three days.

Then we had seven years of peace. I even had two part-time jobs. My middle son found out the truth from his older brother and eventually confessed to what we had done. By then, all three of my boys had finished highschool and had started their adult lives. I even had a young grandchild by the time the confession happened.

I was worried our explanation wouldn't hold up when social services questioned us. But we stuck by our story and told them he had just disappeared. No one thought it was a fabrication. Police initially investigated him as a missing person. We had several years of peace until my middle son confessed. The case was then reopened as a homicide. Investigators, with the help of a dive team, found the body, the rifle and the truck." (end of taping)

Epilogue

The son who assisted her was sentenced to three years in prison following his guilty plea in creating an indignity to human remains. After serving six months, he was granted four monthly unescorted temporary absences of up to 72 hours. He was granted full parole one year later.

After three years behind bars, his mother is now out on day parole. She must reside at a specified residence and any plans to leave the residence must be approved. After six months she will be released for full parole. She must report all sexual and non-sexual relationships and friendships with men to her parole officer as well as any changes to the status of her relationships with others.

Her parole officer reports she has seen "tremendous growth" during her three years behind bars. The Appeal Court considers her to have symptoms of "battered woman syndrome," a psychological condition that can develop from being continually abused by an intimate partner.

During her incarceration, she had voluntarily participated in several initiatives including a women's engagement program, a healthy relationships program, behavioural therapy and psychological counselling.

As the Appeal Court noted, "Due to your history of abuse, concern for your children, depression and learned helplessness, you felt you could not leave the relationship."

In its decision, the board also considered her alcohol use as a result of the abusive relationship, including a suicide attempt. The board also said it considered her to have a very low risk of reoffending, adding that it does not believe her to be "criminally entrenched by any means. The conditions for her release are deemed reasonable and necessary in order to protect society and to facilitate her successful reintegration into the community.

Author's Bio

"As a writer of fiction, I am a constant observer of people and how we behave. How are groups or partnerships formed? What brings people together for marriage? Why is solitude so rewarding for others? It's all pretty captivating.

As a painter, my favourite genre is the examination of the domestic setting. I realize my figurative works have become a natural offshoot of my writings or maybe it's the other way around."

Hazel Harris